TO BREATHE AGAIN

TO BREATHE AGAIN

•

Glen Ebisch

AVALON BOOKS
NEW YORK

ROM
E167 to

For Robert and Lenore Sauer

Chapter One

"**B**reathe, breathe, breathe," Summyr urged. "Remember to relax the belly first and let it fill, then allow the breath to move up into the chest. *Prajna* is the Sanskrit word for breath, but it also stands for the universal force that keeps you and everything else alive. Come into harmony with it."

She opened her eyes after a few breaths and looked out at the five women sitting before her in cross-legged postures on the carpeted floor. Five was a pretty good crowd for her Monday morning yoga class, but three of them were local college students who couldn't be depended on to return next week.

There were only two regulars. One was Janet Benson, a widow in her fifties who had been taking several classes every week for the last six months to help her back pain at the recommendation of her chiropractor.

1

The other potential regular, who had been coming for almost a month now, was Alicia Molloy, a stunning redhead in her late twenties who had clearly taken some yoga before. She came to a number of different classes each week. When Summyr, curious at her open schedule, had asked what she did for a living, Alicia had said she was self-employed and given her a look that discouraged further questions.

"Keep your thoughts focused on your breathing. Let go of any concerns or worries. Remain in the here and now."

I wish that I could follow my own advice, Summyr thought, feeling slightly guilty that her own mind had wandered to other things. *But these morning classes just don't bring in enough students. I have to find some way to offer more classes in the late afternoon or at night.*

The Tuesday and Thursday night classes, which started at six-thirty, were packed to overflowing. She'd even had to restrict the types of postures that could be done because people were bumping into each other.

But how can I add classes after six when I need my other job to help pay for the operation costs of the yoga center? If I quit my job to teach at night, I lose the center. If I keep working at night and rely on these tiny day classes, I lose the center. Summyr felt her own breathing lose its natural rhythm. She tried to relax.

Her breath had just begun to return to the natural in and out, where the entire process seemed effortless, when she heard the door creak. A late-comer! Summyr opened her eyes. A man stood in the doorway. Since the light was behind him, Summyr couldn't make out his face. He took a tentative step into the room.

"Shoes!" Janet Benson, who was sitting nearest the door, said. Her stage whisper caused everyone to open their eyes in alarm.

The man quickly withdrew the foot that had just touched down on the carpet as if the floor were on fire.

Summyr got to her feet. After advising everyone to keep breathing, she walked over to the man, who by now had retreated a few steps backward into the small lobby which also served as her office.

"Hi, my name is Summyr Fox," she said, sticking out her hand after carefully closing the door to the classroom behind her.

"Steven Rafferty," the man replied, taking her hand in his. "Call me Steve."

Since he was about three inches taller than her own five-ten, Summyr had to look up to see into the brown eyes that were surveying her now with a mixture of interest and amusement. His thick brown hair and sturdy features gave him a kind of rugged handsomeness which was increased rather than diminished by a new-looking scar that ran partway down his left cheek. He gave her a broad smile that made him look like a friendly pirate. He was probably about thirty, she guessed, a couple of years older than herself.

"Sorry if I interrupted the class. I meant to get here on time, but the traffic over the bridge into Eastfield is something fierce."

"No problem. If you'll just leave your shoes out here, you can take a mat and pillow from the corner," she said, pointing behind him. "After class I'll have you fill out a physical evaluation form. Do you have any physical limitations?"

Since it was a warm spring day, he was wearing only shorts and a T-shirt. Doesn't seem to be any physical problem there, Summyr thought to herself, glancing quickly at his broad shoulders and well-muscled chest. Not thinking, she had moved on to the way his long brown hair curled gently at the nape of his neck when he surprised her with a response.

"I just had surgery on my left shoulder about a month ago. My physical therapist suggested that some yoga exercises might help."

"Oh," Summyr said, taking a moment to recover. "Well, of course, they might. We can talk after class, but be careful with any of the postures that involve the shoulders. You shouldn't do anything that causes pain. I'll suggest modifications for you as we go along."

Summyr followed Steve into the classroom and returned to her spot at the front of the room. Once he had spread his mat on the floor and sat in imitation of the others, who were still doing yoga breathing or at least pretending to, Summyr led the group through a series of neck stretches. When she moved into a "threading the needle" posture, which involved a great deal of stretching for the shoulder, she went over and sat down next to Steve.

"You might want to do the "child" posture instead,"

Summyr said, sitting down so she was back on her heels, then bending forward until her chest touched her thighs. She placed her arms out on either side of her legs. "This is actually a very relaxing posture."

"I'm sure it is," he said a bit doubtfully. "Once you get used to it."

Slowly he followed her example.

"How is it?" Summyr whispered.

"Not too bad," he replied with a slight gasp. "A little hard to breathe."

"You'll get used to it."

Summyr led the group through a series of both seated and lying down postures. Finally she had everyone stand.

"Now we'll do the forward bend. We'll do it from the "jackknife" position."

She put her hands out from her sides in a T-formation with the palms facing downward. Out of the corner of her eye, she saw Steve begin to raise both arms, then wince and lower the left arm halfway.

"Only go as far as you can," she said to the class in general so as not to embarrass him. "Anyone with shoulder problems can place their hand on their hip."

She then began to lean forward, keeping her arms out to the sides. When her upper body was parallel to the floor, she told the class to lower their arms until their hands reached down as far as they could go, whether it was to their shins, their ankles, or their feet. Moving slowly and deliberately, Summyr reached forward until her palms were flat on the floor, her legs completely straight.

Although yoga practitioners discouraged competition and vanity, Summyr did take pride in her ability to do the postures, or *asanas*, gracefully and fully. Tall and gangly, even as a child, her parents had always urged her not to be ashamed of being taller than the other girls and many of the boys. Like the nonconformists they were, they had encouraged her to stand out from the crowd and not be ashamed of being noticed for her uniqueness. However, it had taken until about five years ago, when she had begun studying yoga, for Summyr to start to become truly comfortable with her body.

Summyr slowly straightened with her hands on her hips. Her eyes met Steve's as he too straightened, and she caught a look of appreciation in his eyes. She started to smile, then remembered that she was the teacher, so a certain amount of formality was necessary. She turned the smile into a nod of encouragement as he completed the posture with relatively good form.

Summyr glanced at the clock, surprised to see that it was already eleven-fifteen. Time always flew by when she was teaching class. She quickly brought the students down into a "corpse" pose where they lay on their backs with their hands and feet splayed out to the side. The last few minutes of class were always devoted to deep relaxation, which was a combination of meditation and the absorption of all that had been learned from practicing the postures.

All of the students except Steve covered themselves with blankets that they had placed next to their exercise mats because the body often cooled rapidly from lying still after so much exertion. Summyr went out into the lobby and got a blanket for Steve. He jumped slightly in surprise as she placed the blanket over him.

"This will keep you warm," she said softly.

He looked up at her and their eyes met. Summyr felt herself blush. She covered students all the time, thinking nothing of it, but this was somehow different. Putting a blanket over this stranger seemed surprisingly intimate.

"Thank you," he whispered.

"You're welcome," she replied in a shaky voice, barely able to restrain herself from gently patting his arm as her hands left the blanket.

After ten minutes of relaxation, Summyr brought the class back to the cross-legged position and led them in chanting "om." Then, after bowing to each member of the class as a sign of respect, the group got to their feet with various degrees of difficulty and began to carry their pillows, mats, and blankets out to the lobby. The three college girls left first, talking excitedly to each other about some upcoming event.

Alicia Molloy got to her feet gracefully and with a slight nod at Summyr walked across the floor, heading toward the lobby. Summyr noticed that Steve Rafferty's eyes never left Alicia as she strolled across the room. Summyr couldn't really blame him; the woman exuded a sort of cool sex appeal that she imagined most men would find irresistible. Although enough men had told Summyr that she was pretty over the years to convince her that it might be true, she knew that what Alicia had went well beyond that. Perhaps it was her aloofness, which bordered on self-absorption, that served as an unspoken challenge to the opposite sex. "Try to get me to notice you, if you dare," she seemed to be saying with her walk and the very slant of her head.

"That was a very nice class, Summyr," Janet Benson said, slowly climbing to her feet.

"How's your back today?" Summyr asked.

"Well, I may not look it in comparison with the others," the woman said, glancing at Alicia with envious eyes, "but I'm actually a lot more flexible than I was even a month ago. And compared to six months ago, it's been a miracle. My back doesn't ache nearly as much, and the pains in my abdomen have let up, too. My chiropractor thinks that as my muscles get stronger, a lot of my problems will disappear."

"I'm sure he's right. But stay within your limitations. Don't try to do too much, too soon."

"Don't worry," the woman said with a chuckle, "I'm not going to try to keep up with you young people."

As she turned away from Janet Benson, Summyr saw that Steve was standing by the window in the lobby looking out at the parking lot. She went over and stood next to him. He was watching as Alicia Molloy left the building and got into her car. Although a bit annoyed at his fascination with the redhead, Summyr decided to take the diplomatic approach.

"She's very attractive," she commented.

"Yes, I guess she is," he replied uncertainly. Then

he turned to her and smiled. "Probably as vain as heck."

Summyr felt a silly grin of relief slip onto her face, but suppressed it.

"We shouldn't assume bad things about people just because they're beautiful."

"Of course not, I'm not assuming anything bad about you," he replied with a glint in his eye.

"That's because I'm not beautiful," Summyr said, turning away in confusion and looking down at her desk. "Let me have you fill out the medical form."

She slowly took a medical form out of her file box, attached it to a clipboard, and grabbed a pen. She concentrated carefully on each step, focusing her mind until her chaotic emotions were completely under control. No one had talked to her that way in over a year. Not since John had died. And she wasn't certain that she was ready for that kind of conversation even now. All the clever boy-and-girl talk had disappeared from her life in an instant, and she wasn't ready to risk reliving that kind of pain.

When she looked up to hand Steve the form, he was standing in front of the desk, rubbing his sore shoulder absentmindedly, and staring at her. He waited a moment until Janet Benson had waved goodbye and gone down the stairs before speaking.

"Look, that was stupid of me. I was trying to be smart. My mistake. You could be married, or engaged, or be going out with some guy you've known since you were in fifth grade. I shouldn't have spoken to you like that without knowing you better. After all, we've only just met."

Summyr shrugged as if none of it mattered.

"So are you?"

"Am I what?"

"Engaged, married, or in a long-term relationship with the guy next door."

"No. I was engaged once," Summyr heard herself say, finding it hard to believe that she was revealing her past to this stranger.

"But you broke up."

She shook her head, feeling the familiar tears start to burn at the back of her eyes.

"He died," she said hoarsely, and thrust the clipboard out at Steve as if to prevent him from intruding any further on her privacy.

He took it from her hands. "I'm sorry," he said. "How long ago?"

"Almost a year and a half."

"How did it happen?"

"Rock climbing. John was an accountant, and he enjoyed having a hobby that got him out from behind a desk. He was in Colorado on his vacation when it happened."

"Were you there?"

Summyr shook her head. "I don't climb. And I . . . well, I didn't really want him to go."

"Yeah, relationships require a lot of compromises."

Not sure whether he meant that she should have accompanied John to Colorado, or that John should have changed hobbies, Summyr gave him a neutral nod.

"Is this what you do for a living?" he asked, surveying the yoga studio.

"I'm trying," Summyr said.

"Yeah, it must be hard to get a business of your own off the ground."

She nodded. "I work part-time at a health-food store to help make ends meet."

"I guess the basic concept of health food fits in with yoga," he said.

She studied his face to see if he was making fun of her. Some of the men she had dated were sarcastic when she told them what she did for a living. There were lots of adolescent jokes about the fruits-and-nuts crowd. Steve smiled, but he didn't seem to be making fun of her.

She nodded, and he turned his attention to the form. A few minutes later he handed it back to her.

"That should do it."

Summyr looked it over carefully. He lived in town and gave his age as thirty. His employer was listed as something named MediCorp.

"You had arthroscopic surgery on your shoulder eight weeks ago. What happened?"

"Car accident. Some guy had too much to drink and came across onto my side of the road. I went off the shoulder and rolled the car. Tore the heck out of my shoulder. That's where I got this, too," he said, stroking the scar on the side of his face. "The doctor says it will fade some after a while. But I might need plastic surgery if I want my old handsome face back. What do you think? Would it be worth it?" he asked with a boyish grin.

"Maybe the universe was trying to tell you something about being vain," Summyr replied, smiling to take the sting out of the remark..

The man laughed. "I deserved that. Never fish for compliments, my mother always says, you don't know what you'll catch."

"How many times a week are you planning to take yoga?"

"The physical therapist said that I should come at least twice a week if I want to make any real progress."

Summyr nodded her agreement and handed him a membership form. "If you take an unlimited membership for a month you can attend as many classes as you want, day or evening. Will your work allow you to come regularly during the day?"

He paused for a moment. "Yeah. I sell drugs."

Summyr's eyebrows rose.

"The legal kind. I go around to doctor's offices and tell them about the new pharmaceuticals our company has coming out. So I can pretty much work my schedule around coming here."

He filled out the membership form and handed her a check. "Do most people attend the same classes every week?"

"Sometimes. Of course, if a person has a change in schedule they may come to a different class."

"I was just wondering if the same people would be here on Wednesday," he said.

Like a certain red-haired person named Alicia, Summyr thought. "Hard to tell," she replied.

"Right," Steven said, sitting down and putting on his shoes. Summyr ignored him, busying herself at her desk.

"See you on Wednesday," he said, standing in front of her desk.

"Yes," Summyr said, not looking up, deciding that practicing some of Alicia's coolness might not be a bad idea.

She heard the door close and allowed her eyes to sweep across the room. The nerve of the guy to compliment her and then try to find out when Alicia would be available. Some guys would flirt with any woman. It was like a reflex response—show me anyone even remotely female and I'll flirt.

Anyway, Summyr thought, as she automatically opened her mail, I've got more important things to worry about than an out-of-control playboy. The rent is due next week, and I've got to find some money to run another ad in the newspaper.

She opened a business envelope that seemed more important than the usual advertisement or bill. When she pulled out the stiff white paper and read the two-paragraph letter, her hands began to shake.

"Oh, great," she muttered. "This is exactly what I need. This is just perfect."

Chapter Two

Uncle Harold looked up at her after reading the letter, his face somber.

"You're scaring me, Uncle," Summyr said.

The letter was from a local lawyer's office and was addressed to Summyr at the Centered Self Yoga Center. The body of the letter was short and to the point.

> *Pleased be advised that Northside Properties, the owners of the building located at 12 Broad Street, Eastfield, Massachusetts, are planning an extensive renovation of the property at that location. These renovations will require that all the current tenants vacate the premises within thirty days of the date of this letter.*

"I'm sorry, but it looks like you'll have to move," he said.

"Are you saying that there's nothing I can do?" asked Summyr. "I thought I had a three-year lease."

Her uncle shook his head. "Your lease requires that the landlord give you thirty days notice to break it, which is exactly what he's doing. If you remember when you signed the lease, I mentioned that usually you'd be guaranteed the three years, but this was a building that was awaiting further development, so they could ask you to leave with only a month's notice."

"Which was why the rent was so low," Summyr said.

Uncle Harold nodded his head and smiled sadly. "I'm afraid that you get what you pay for in these matters."

Summyr sighed and looked out through the window next to the desk. She could see the forsythia pushing its cascades of yellow flowers up against the glass. Her uncle had his practice in an old colonial house that dated back to the middle of the eighteenth century. Summyr often joked that none of the walls were plumb and none of the bushes were trimmed. Her Uncle would smile and say that he couldn't do anything about the walls, and he wouldn't hire a new landscaper who actually worked until the old man who had been doing the job for fifty years retired or died.

Uncle Harold had a heart of gold, and Summyr didn't want him unnecessarily worrying about this rental problem or feeling that it was his fault.

"Oh, well," she said, "I guess I'll just have to find somewhere else for the studio."

Her uncle's face became even more morose. "That may not be easy. Commercial properties are in short supply right now. For the kind of space you'll need, I'm afraid you'll have to pay substantially more."

"And I can barely afford what the current space is costing me."

Her uncle's jowls came down over his collar as he directed his glance at his desk. He never looked her in the eye when he was about to say something that might embarrass her.

"Perhaps if you would allow me to provide some financial assistance. . . . just until you get the business on its feet."

Summyr shook her head. "I appreciate the offer, Uncle, but you know that I couldn't do that."

It wasn't just that she valued her independence, although that certainly entered into it. Her father, Sam, and his only brother, Harold, had been competing forces in her life since her mother had died five years ago. Summyr remained careful not to allow either one to have too much influence on her life. Her father, who had managed to make a decent, if not lavish, living as a musician for over thirty years, had recently moved to Florida, where he was now the resident musician and entertainment director at a senior citizen community. He kept urging Summyr to join him as his assistant, a job offer she had so far resisted.

Uncle Harold had been almost as in love with her mother Miriam as her father was, and he had always considered Sam, his younger brother by two years, to be a shiftless bohemian who had never provided adequately for Summyr or her mother. This may have been true by Harold's middle-class standards, but they had never wanted for food or an adequate roof over their heads. As her mother often said, Harold could provide food for the body, but it was Sam who provided food for the soul. Whatever Harold's limitations, Summyr knew that he loved her like a daughter. To live her own life, however, she had to steer a course between the dual forces of Sam and Harold.

Her uncle cleared his throat and spoke as if he had read her mind. "Sam would never have to know."

"But I would know, Uncle Harold."

"Yes . . . well. What will you do then?"

She paused. She was already working at Root and Branch afternoons and evenings on Mondays, Wednesdays, and Fridays. Chrissy Chandler, who was the assistant manager at the organic food store, had helped her get the job a few months after Summyr opened the yoga center two years ago. In exchange, Summyr had given Chrissy a lifetime free membership for yoga classes. Maybe, Summyr thought, she could add some hours at the store on Saturday after her morning yoga class. But would that be enough to cover a large increase in rent? Probably not. The local Y had wanted her to teach a class for them, as had the hospital in town. Maybe, just maybe, she could put together enough small jobs to pay the rent on a new yoga space.

"Perhaps you should consider getting a full-time

job. Yoga is a wonderful hobby, but it may not be a feasible way to make a living," her uncle said.

Summyr bit back an angry response. Uncle Harold was only expressing what most reasonable people would say. A women in her late twenties with no husband and little capital couldn't expect to be successful at launching a small business, especially one that only appealed to a relatively small portion of the population. But deep down she thought that yoga was beneficial both physically and mentally for lots of people if only they knew about it and were encouraged to give it a chance.

"I may have to do that," she replied. "But I'm going to try everything else I can first to keep the yoga center open. I have thirty days. Something may turn up before then."

Her uncle smiled at her affectionately. "I admire your optimism. Wish I had more if it myself. But sometimes life does give us lemons."

"And we have to make lemonade. Yes, I know that. But sometimes the universe supplies answers to our problems as well, if we give it a chance."

"Well, just in case the universe doesn't come through for you this time, remember that I'm here to help. If you won't accept money, I can at least give you some help in finding a job if you decide you want one."

Summyr stood up, and as her uncle came around from behind the desk, she gave him a huge hug.

"I won't forget," she said.

"Be sure that you don't," he said. "After all, aside

from that rascally brother of mine, you're the only family I've got. And if a man can't help his family. . . ."

"Then who can he help?" Summyr said, finishing one of her uncle's favorite sayings.

As she walked out to her car, Summyr thought again how wonderful her Uncle Harold was. She was glad that by having dinner with him every couple of weeks and getting together on holidays she was able to make his life a bit less lonely. Even though her father was alone as well, she knew that wherever he lived he would be surrounded by laughing, singing people and have a crowd of friends. What Uncle Harold needed was a wife, thought Summyr. But that would happen only if he got over his memories of her mother.

Summyr was still thinking about her uncle's situation when she pulled into the parking lot in front of Root and Branch. She spotted Richie Rivero's red sports car parked right in front of the door as usual. Although Richie was the manager of Root and Branch, even on a good day he rarely showed up for more than an hour, and usually only came to make sure that the shipments had been delivered for Chrissy and Summyr to unpack.

When Summyr walked in the front door, she saw that nothing had changed. Richie was standing in the middle of an aisle, leaning against a display rack for support, as if the effort of remaining upright was too much for him.

He smiled when he saw Summyr. "How you

doin'?" he asked, giving her what he no doubt thought was a charming smile.

Summyr nodded. Richie was slender and an inch or two shorter than she was. Flirting seemed to be second nature to him, and he never said anything to a woman that didn't sound like it should be followed up with a wink and a smirk. Although he was quite good-looking, in Summyr's opinion he wasn't nearly handsome enough to compensate for his personality.

"Right down here, sweetheart," Richie called, as Chrissy appeared at the far end of the aisle with a box under each arm. He pointed at an empty section of the shelves, but didn't make any effort to give her a hand.

Giving Richie a disgusted look, which he didn't seem to notice, Summyr rushed down the aisle and grabbed one of the boxes from Chrissy just before it slipped from under her arm.

"Thanks," Chrissy said, pushing her long stringy hair back out of her face. "These are pretty heavy."

"What's in them?"

"Wheat flour. I already brought in the boxes of bulgur and rice. This is the last load."

"Richie should have given you a hand," Summyr whispered.

"Well, he isn't really dressed for work. You know, there's always some flour on the outside of these boxes," Chrissy said, looking down at her denim skirt which had turned a dusty gray.

Standing there in his black jeans and navy turtleneck, Richie certainly wasn't dressed for work, thought Summyr, but that was how he always dressed.

It was virtually a uniform with Richie, and it always supplied him with a handy excuse for not working.

Between the two of them, the woman cut open the boxes and placed the bags of flour on the shelves, while Richie stood behind them making occasional suggestions as to how they should be displayed. Finally, the three of them stood back and surveyed the shelf.

"Well, I'm glad that's done," Richie said, brushing imaginary dirt from his sweater. "I've got to go out now. If those flyers come in later, you'll see that they go up front, honey?"

Chrissy nodded eagerly, looking up at Richie with adoring puppy eyes.

"And you'd better let Summyr take the cash register until you get yourself cleaned up," Richie said, giving Chrissy a critical once-over.

Chrissy made desperate slapping motions at her skirt and tried to pull her hair away from her sweating forehead.

"Remember girls, ninety percent of selling is based on appearance. If the customers are impressed by you, they'll be impressed by your product," Richie intoned, sharing another saying Summyr knew he'd gotten from the one marketing course he'd taken at a community college.

"Will you be back later, Richie?" Chrissy asked, a hopeful expression obvious on her face.

"You never know, sweetheart, you never know. But if you want to reach me, there's always the old cell phone." He mimed punching numbers into a phone. Then he gave a wave and headed for the door.

"If you want to reach him, there's always a two-by-four to the side of his head," Summyr mumbled.

Chrissy giggled. "Oh, he's not that bad. He just acts that way because he's so insecure. With the right woman to give him confidence, Richie would be just fine."

Summyr nodded and kept her mouth shut. Since she had started working at Root and Branch, she had come to know Chrissy pretty well. They'd been acquaintances more than real friends in high school, thrown together because their fathers were both musicians. Chrissy's father taught music at the local middle school, and occasionally did gigs with Sam's band when he needed extra musicians.

Short and heavyset, Chrissy had always worn clothes that did nothing to enhance her appearance. Summyr had wondered about this until she had met Chrissy's mother and found that she dressed in an identical way. Summyr's infrequent suggestions to Chrissy as to how she might improve her appearance were always met with hurt looks and comments about how "the inner woman was more important than mere appearances." Since Summyr half-believed this herself, she always backed off.

But to see Richie so blatantly exploiting Chrissy's desire to be liked made her angry. Summyr wasn't sure whether she was more upset at Richie for doing it or at Chrissy for letting him. Chrissy was far more naive than any woman in her late twenties had a right to be today, but that just made Summyr feel protective toward her. She had to find some way to deal with Chrissy's unhealthy attraction to Richie.

"How did your class go this morning?" Chrissy asked a few minutes later when she returned from the back room, having now managed to spread the flour dust evenly over both her skirt and blouse.

Summyr explained about the letter from Northside Properties, and her uncle's view that little could be done about it.

"You aren't going to give up on the yoga center, are you?" Chrissy asked.

"I may not have a choice." Having a business of her own had always been one of Chrissy's dreams, and Summyr knew that Chrissy admired her for taking a chance and giving it a try. The thought of disappointing Chrissy somehow made it all seem worse.

"You could put in more hours here if that would help. We could use two people on Saturday afternoons, that's one of our busiest times. Richie doesn't care; he lets me pretty much run things anyway. As long as he can show the owners that we're making a good profit, he's happy."

Summyr gave her friend's arm a squeeze. "Thanks. I think I'll take you up on the offer. But even if I put in more hours here and teach extra classes, I'm still not sure that I'll be able to afford a new studio. The place where I am now is awfully cheap compared with anything else I'm likely to find."

"No offense. But there's a good reason for that."

Summyr nodded. "I know. The place isn't much, but the price is right."

Her current center was on the second floor above what had originally been a small warehouse. The upper floor had been used as offices for the trucking company that operated out of the warehouse below. After the trucking company went out of business, the owners of the building had rented the second floor to Summyr. The first floor remained empty: a cavernous space filled with rows of empty shelves. To reach Summyr's studio you had to enter the warehouse, then climb a long flight of exposed stairs to the second floor. Not exactly a convenient arrangement, nor suitable to most businesses, facts that had probably led to the extremely low rent.

"You've only got a month to look around and find what might be available. I'll keep my eyes and ears open and see what I can find," Chrissy said helpfully.

"Thanks. By the way, I got a new student in the class today. A guy."

Chrissy's face brightened. "You don't get many of those."

That was true, Summyr admitted to herself, nine out of ten students were women. If only there were a way to convince more guys that flexibility was just as important as strength and big muscles. When she had run track and field in high school, she'd seen lots of guys injured because their muscles were too tight due to overtraining. But you could never get guys to take the time and be patient enough to stretch properly.

"What's this guy like?" Chrissy asked. "Is he young?"

"Thirty."

"Is he cute?"

Summyr paused. "He's certainly attractive. He has thick brown hair and perfect teeth, but cute makes him sound too pretty. There's a scar on his cheek and his nose is slightly crooked, like it may have been broken once. I guess I'd say he looks rugged."

"Like a cowboy," Chrissy said, getting a kind of misty look in her eyes.

Summyr smiled. "There aren't many cowboys in Massachusetts."

"What kind of work does he do?"

Summyr explained that he worked for a drug company and told the story of how he had been in an automobile accident.

"You know," Chrissy said in a confidential whisper, "they say that men are most vulnerable when they're recovering from an injury. That's when they really crave love and attention. If you could help Steve on the road to recovery, who knows what might happen."

Summyr wondered what magazine had provided Chrissy with this piece of information. She could imagine the article now: "Follow the Ambulance and Get Your Man."

"We'll see. I hardly know him, and anyway, he seems to have his sights set on Alicia Molloy."

Chrissy grunted. She had seen Alicia in class once and taken an instant dislike to her based on appearance and attitude.

"She may look like a fashion model, but she's cold. Don't get discouraged, with your personality you'll have Steve eating out of your hand in no time."

A silly picture flashed through Summyr's mind of herself in a gauzy white dress sitting on a rock in the forest. Her outstretched hand held some kind of seed. Steve was crawling toward her on his hands and knees with a doelike expression on his face.

"I'm not sure that I'm interested," Summyr said.

"You paid enough attention to his appearance. You must be a little interested," said Chrissy with uncharacteristic insight.

Summyr caught herself blushing and busied herself straightening the rack of vitamins on the counter in front of her.

"You know it's been over a year now since John . . ." Chrissy let the rest of the sentence trail off as she saw Summyr shake her head at the sound of his name.

"I've heard all the good advice on that subject," Summyr said shortly. "I don't need to hear it again."

There was a quick intake of breath from Chrissy. Summyr knew that she had gone too far.

"I was just trying to be helpful," Chrissy said a moment later in a hurt tone.

"I know you were," Summyr said. She turned toward her friend and gave her a hug. "It's not your fault if I'm not ready to listen to good advice."

I wonder if I'll ever be, she thought to herself.

Chapter Three

The next morning, promptly at a quarter to ten, Summyr again pulled into the parking lot of Root and Branch. She put her car in a space in the middle of the lot, away from the front of the store. "Always leave the good spaces for the customers," Richie insisted.

Summyr might have agreed with him on this one, except for the fact that Root and Branch was in a large strip mall with hundreds of spaces, so parking was never a problem. Besides, on Richie's rare personal appearances he always parked right in front of the store if there was a space.

Selecting the right key on the ring, she let herself in the front door and switched on the lights. She then relocked the door because the first ten minutes were given over to organizing the store, and she didn't want customers walking in on her. Although it was early spring, it still got chilly in the store overnight, so Summyr went to the rear of the shop and pushed up the thermostat. Then she went into the back room and checked the list of deliveries due for the day. The trucks pulled around to the back where there was a small loading dock.

She was relieved to see that nothing was due in this morning. Since she was alone in the store all morning, it would have been difficult if large deliveries had arrived. Some drivers refused to bring boxes of goods inside the store and would only carry them as far as the dock. It was a challenge to watch the front of the store and haul in merchandise at the same time. One delivery was scheduled for this afternoon, but Chrissy would be there to help by then.

After setting up the cash register, she opened the front door. On Tuesdays there were usually very few customers until after eleven, so Summyr busied herself putting merchandise on the shelves and re-marking some items due to go on sale. Soon she had developed a rhythm. When the bell over the door rang, Summyr was so lost in her own thoughts about the future of her yoga center that she didn't even notice.

"Hello Summyr," a familiar voice said.

Summyr looked down the aisle to the front of the shop. Since the light was in her eyes from the large front windows, she couldn't clearly see who it was.

"It's me, Janet Benson," the woman said.

As Summyr walked closer, she recognized the woman from her morning yoga class, looking rather more fashionable than she did in class when she wore her baggy sweats. She had on a violet blouse with heather green slacks that made her look very youthful for a woman in her late fifties. Chrissy had mentioned that Mrs. Benson came in on a regular basis, but Summyr had never seen her in the store before.

"Hi," Summyr said, "it's nice to see you here. I heard that you came in frequently, but usually not while I'm working."

"Actually, I make a point of coming in while Chrissy is here." Realizing how that sounded, Mrs. Benson gave an embarrassed smile. "I'm not trying to avoid you, it's just that I like to talk to Chrissy."

"I didn't know you and Chrissy were friends."

"We met a while back in one of your yoga classes. I think it must have been on a day when the store was closed for a holiday. We happened to sit next to each other and started to talk."

"Chrissy is easy to talk to."

Janet Benson nodded and stared at the shelves for a moment.

"Is there something I can help you find?"

"There's no easy way to ease into this, so I'm just going to plow right ahead. 'Be direct' is my motto."

"Okay," Summyr said, wondering where all this was going.

"I came in today specifically to see you because I know you're a friend of Chrissy's. We have to do something about her."

"How do you mean?"

"Have you met that jerk, Richie, who runs this place?"

Summyr was considering how to answer the question diplomatically when Mrs. Benson continued.

"Of course you have—what am I saying—he's your boss, too. But I can't imagine that you're as enamored of him as poor Chrissy is."

"No, I'm not."

"And you can't think that Chrissy's infatuation with that lazy excuse for a manager is healthy."

Mrs. Benson had gotten red in the face during her tirade and paused to catch her breath.

"Would you like a cup of tea?" Summyr asked, leading the woman toward the back of the store where they kept hot water ready with open boxes of various teas to sample.

It had been Chrissy's idea to make the samples available. In the face of Richie's opposition that they would just be getting ripped off by their customers, Chrissy had said, "People are afraid to try new things. But once you can convince them to give it a chance, they'll probably like it. In the long run you'll make back many times more than the samples cost." The idea of increased profits at no greater effort to himself had won Richie over.

Summyr put a bag of one of the more calming teas into a cup of hot water and handed it to Janet. She took a slightly stronger one for herself. She didn't want to get too relaxed with a day of work yet ahead.

"I'm sorry. But I get so mad when I watch that skinny twerp prance around here like the rooster in a henhouse. And Chrissy seems to think that he's God's gift to womankind."

Summyr smiled at the accurate depiction of Richie. "I know what you're saying, Janet, but I'm not sure what we can do. That's the way Chrissy feels, and she won't listen to anything bad about him. Saying anything negative about Richie just upsets her."

Mrs. Benson sipped her tea.

"This is really good," she said. "Very soothing."

"It's got a little kava in it."

"What's that?"

"An herb that works as a sort of relaxant. But don't worry, there isn't enough in one tea bag to impair your driving."

The woman gave a snort. "Good thing. My driving's bad enough. I've already had the Lexus in the body shop twice in the last year. Nothing major, but the guy who worked on it last was almost begging me to be more careful with such a beautiful machine. Problem is that I start thinking about things and get distracted."

"Remember what we say in class—stay focused on the here and now."

"The here and now for me is doing something about Chrissy. The only way we can get her out of Richie's clutches is to change that girl's way of thinking about herself. You've seen the way she looks: that long stringy hair, the mismatched clothes, the tennis sneakers. Doesn't her mother give her any advice?"

"Her mother dresses the same way," Summyr replied.

"Well, that explains a lot. I always say that if you

start polishing up the outer woman, the inner woman will develop a lot more self-respect."

Summyr paused, not sure whether she wanted to contradict Janet. "I guess I always thought that it was the other way around."

Mrs. Benson gave her a quizzical glance.

"I mean that if a person develops more self-respect, it will influence the way they act and look."

Mrs. Benson considered the possibility. "Okay. Let's say you're right. How are we going to do that for Chrissy?"

"I don't know. Doesn't a person have to be at the point where they want to change before that can happen?"

"I only partly agree with you on that one. Sometimes a person can be partway there, and a little helpful shove from the outside is just what they need."

As an apparent demonstration Mrs. Benson gave a box of stone-ground cornmeal a hard shove and sent it skittering along the shelf.

"I see your point. And you would be that shove from the outside that Chrissy needs."

"Sure, I'm not saying that you haven't tried, but there's only so much a woman can say to another woman who's the same age. What Chrissy needs is some sound advice from someone old enough to be her mother. A little motherly push in the right direction."

Summyr smiled to herself at the thought of what a "little push" from Mrs. Benson would be like.

"But what's the right direction?"

"Yeah, I'm going to have to give that some thought.

On clothes and makeup I could make some suggestions in a flash, but changing the inner woman might take a little more time. But that's okay, now that Frank's gone and my boys are grown, what I've got plenty of is time. I'm going to be giving Chrissy a lot of thought."

The intensity of Janet's expression made Summyr glad that it was Chrissy who was going to be the center of all this attention and not her.

When Chrissy came in at noon, Summyr looked at her more closely than usual and with new eyes. What Mrs. Benson had said was true. Although Chrissy was a bit plump, she increased the bulkiness of her appearance by wearing shapeless jeans clearly designed for someone a couple of sizes larger than her. They were cinched in the middle with an unsightly black leather belt. Her light brown hair was clean, but looked like it had been combed with her fingers and clearly had been allowed to grow without any attempt at style for several years. On her feet she was wearing scuffed white tennis shoes with little white socks that barely reached her ankles, and her blue work shirt was hanging out of the back of her pants as if she had dressed on the run.

Summyr tried to imagine her in better-fitting and more fashionable clothes, sporting a more appropriate hairstyle. She had to admit that the change might be dramatic. But she still thought that this wasn't an issue that could be approached with cosmetic modifications alone. Chrissy's attitude toward herself had to be altered. Summyr remembered that as far back as high school, Chrissy had always been one of those smart but socially unskilled girls, who seemed unable to show others how truly nice and capable she really was.

Mrs. Benson is going to need all her push and lots of luck to make Chrissy into a confident, independent young woman, Summyr thought, as she watched her friend head toward the back room with her shirttail waving behind her like a flag.

The bell over the door rang, and Summyr looked over the display to see who had entered. Steven Rafferty's face came into view.

"Hi," Steve said with a wave. "How are you doing?"

"Fine," she said, surprised to see him.

"I was hoping to find you here," he said, and smiled.

"How did you know where I worked?"

"You told me that you worked in a health-food store. How many health-food stores do you think there are in town?"

"Two."

Steve grinned. "I already tried the other one."

She looked at him, waiting for an explanation as to why he had gone to all the trouble of finding her.

"Uh, I thought that maybe we kind of got off on the wrong foot yesterday. I'm not sure why, but things like that happen sometimes."

She stared, not making it easy for him. He probably wants to take me out so he can get Alicia's number, she thought.

"So I figured that maybe we could go out to dinner tonight if you're free."

"I have a yoga class."

Steve glanced at the clock. "It's almost noon. What time do you get off for lunch? I promise to get you back on time."

"She can go right now," Chrissy said, coming down the aisle with her eyes fixed on Steve.

"Are you the boss?" he asked, sticking out his hand.

"The only one here right now," Chrissy replied, giving his hand a hearty shake.

"But there's a shipment coming in about half an hour," Summyr said weakly.

"Light stuff. Don't worry about it. You and Steve go to lunch. And don't worry about being back right at one. Nothing is going to happen that I can't handle."

Chrissy gave Steve a look that said, "Get this girl out of here and show her a good time." She even took Summyr's jacket off the coat tree and handed it to Steve.

"But don't you have work to do?" Summyr asked Steve.

"All done for the day. My time is my own," he said, helping her on with her jacket. He took her arm gently and led her toward the door, then looked back at Chrissy. "Don't worry, boss, I'll put some good food in her so she'll be able to do lots of hard work in the afternoon."

Chrissy winked, and Summyr felt that somehow the person whose life she was going to change had turned the tables on her.

Chapter Four

"Where are we going?" Summyr asked as Steve headed out on a country road. "You know I do have to work this afternoon."

"Don't worry. We're just going up the road. With all the congestion in the center of town, I thought it would be nice to get a little way out in the country."

Eastfield was a small town in western Massachusetts that over the last two hundred years had gradually spread out from the quaint central town green to include several blocks of shops, two modern industrial parks, and expanding residential areas. It was old enough to have a number of renovated nineteenth-century mills serving as office and business space. There were also early-twentieth-century factories and warehouses, such as the one Summyr's studio was in, that were awaiting remodeling. Although the area around the green was still the hub for restaurants and small shops, the traffic and congested parking made it a difficult spot at lunchtime.

As they headed north, Summyr tried to relax and pay attention to the light green vegetation starting to burst forth on the trees and bushes. Spring was definitely on the way. Not that it was one of the better-defined seasons in New England, often coming late and quickly moving into the heat and humidity of summer, but for a few short weeks, the cool days and the budding plants combined to provide a spirit of optimism and renewal.

Steve turned up a narrow gravel road that appeared to lead nowhere.

"Where are we going?" Summyr asked suspiciously.

"You'll see," Steve said with a smile,

They reached the top of the hill and swung around a bend. In front of them was a large white house sitting on a small rise. A weathered white shingle sign hung from a post.

"The General Knox Inn," Summyr read. "I've heard of this place, but I've never eaten here."

"I've been here a couple of times. The food is pretty good and the view is tremendous."

As a child Summyr had only eaten out at places like these when her father got complimentary meals because he was performing. That was usually at larger restaurants with banquet halls for weddings, graduations, and bar mitzvahs. In her teens and early twenties, she had usually gone with friends to local clubs, and John had always preferred steak houses. So although she had lived in the area most of her life, her knowledge of small, expensive restaurants was limited.

They entered through the front door, which sported an elaborate wood surround, and walked into the finely polished oak front hall. A well-dressed older woman greeted them and Steve gave his name. She immediately led them down the hall to a spacious room in the back and seated them by a window with a panoramic view.

Summyr held the menu in her hand without reading it. She stared out the window at the sloping green lawn that disappeared into the woods where a brook flashed in the sunlight. As her eyes moved up to the tops of the trees, she saw the mountains, which looked close enough to touch and showed a light covering of green, as though they were in the process of dressing for the summer.

She glanced away from the view and saw Steve looking at her. He smiled as though he enjoyed seeing her take in the new experience.

"Great spot, isn't it?" he said.

"Magnificent."

"It looks really great, too, in the winter when the hills are covered with snow. And of course you can't beat the colors in the fall. And the summer isn't bad either." He gave a small laugh. "I guess we'll have to try it in all the seasons."

"You seem pretty sure of yourself."

"How's that?"

"Well, first of all you made a reservation, so you must have been pretty confident that I would come to lunch with you."

Steve shrugged. "Reservations can always be cancelled. Without one, we'd never get this table."

Summyr glanced around at the crowded dining room and realized that he was right.

"And now you're saying that we'll have lunch together many times in the future."

He leaned across the table, his expression serious. "I want you to know that I don't go out with someone just to have something to do. Things may not work out, but I always start out on the assumption that the first date is the beginning of something more lasting. Don't you think that way, too?"

Summyr paused. "Yes, I guess I do. That's why I usually don't go out with someone unless I know them pretty well."

She had met John when he helped her uncle during tax season. Uncle Harold had suggested that they meet, and it was only after a number of tentative conversations in her Uncle Harold's stuffy law library that they had gone out on their first date.

"So you're breaking your rule for me," Steve said. "You hardly know me at all."

"No. I'm breaking it for Chrissy. She obviously wanted me to go out with you, so here I am. It had nothing to do with you."

"I see." He grinned as if he didn't believe her at all. "What are you going to have? I never thought to ask if you might be a vegetarian. Do you only eat tofu and bean sprouts? I'm afraid that I don't see any of that on the menu."

"No tofu and bean sprouts. What a shame!" Summyr said with mock horror. "Well, I guess I'll just have to make due with the flounder stuffed with crab meat."

"Do you only eat things that swim and not those that walk around on land?"

"I eat all kinds of meat. I've even been known to consume the occasional sirloin, but I don't make a habit of it. I eat a sensible, balanced diet."

"You are what you eat, is that the idea?"

Summyr considered that for a moment. "I'd say you are what you think, and a bad diet leads to bad thoughts."

Steve raised a skeptical eyebrow. "Well, I'll try it your way this time and go with the scrod."

His eyes were hazel, and the little creases beside them showed that he laughed a lot. But one of the creases disappeared into the scar on his left cheek. That wouldn't have been a laughing matter, thought Summyr.

"I'll bet that hurt," she said, staring at the injured side of his face.

"Actually, I hardly realized what had happened at the time, until I saw all the blood. But it sure started to hurt later."

"It's scary when you think that you can be driving down the street, minding your own business, and something like that can happen."

"That's the way life is," Steve said, as the waitress stopped at the table and took their order.

When the waitress left, he took a sip of water and studied Summyr speculatively over the rim.

"What are you thinking?" she asked.

"I was wondering what it is that you look for in a man."

Summyr laughed. "There are so many things, I wouldn't know where to begin. I have extremely high standards."

"Well, let me put it another way then," Steven said. "What was the primary characteristic that attracted you to your fiancé?"

That Steve would ask her about John took Summyr by surprise. Even her friends avoided mentioning him after the funeral, and the subject of his death was always given a wide berth. Sometimes Summyr felt that people would rather pretend that he had never been alive and a part of her life than bring up a painful subject. Although it was essentially kindness on their part, it had left her to deal with the pain of his death by herself and in silence.

"His stability," she heard herself say without hesitation.

Surprised at the certainty in her voice, she realized that it really had been John's stability that had attracted her to him.

Steve looked at her quizzically.

"John was a planner. He knew exactly why he was doing what he was doing and where he intended to be in the next five years. He worked for a large accounting firm and was already working his way up the ladder."

"And that's what you're looking for in a man?" he asked, sounding incredulous.

"Why is that so surprising? Isn't that what every woman is supposed to want?"

"Some women, maybe. But not ones who teach yoga and spell their names funny."

Summyr grinned. "That's probably why I do. When your parents are unreconstructed hippies who spend their lives making music and granola bars, you long for a little order and predictability in your life."

"So why aren't you working in an office behind a computer screen? You could be pulling down a regular salary and putting lots of money in a pension plan."

"Now there's a question I ask myself almost every day," Summyr said. She looked out at the hills to avoid Steve's careful gaze.

"And how do you answer yourself?" he prodded, after several seconds had passed.

She turned back to him. "I'm my parents' child, I guess. I went to community college and got my associate's degree in business, but there's a side of me that wants to do what my mom wanted to do. A part of me that will never sell out just to have money and security."

"So you look for that in a partner instead. Let the man carry the load of being boring and pedestrian, while you lead a life of spontaneity and creativity."

Although he was smiling, there was an edge to his voice that indicated he was deeply serious about the point he was making. Her initial reaction was to vehemently deny his charge, but then her last conversation with John came back to her. She had been asking—virtually begging—him not to go on his trip.

"This is the one exciting thing that I do in my life, Summyr, you can't expect me to give that up. Not even for you," he had said, throwing his clothes in a suitcase.

"But I'm worried about what might happen," she said.

John had turned and put his arms around her. "I know you are, and I'm sorry." He had kissed her gently. Then as she stood in the middle of the room, her head down, he had walked out the door. She had never seen him alive again.

She came back to the present. "I don't want a man who's not creative—he can paint, sculpt, write, or crochet afghans for all I care. But if he sky dives, bungee jumps, races cars, or endangers his life on a regular basis in any other way, then count me out. I've been through that once. I'm not going to go through it again."

"I see," Steve said hesitantly. "Well, I can certainly understand why you would feel that way."

"Do you have any dangerous hobbies?" Summyr asked suspiciously.

"Not at all. I spend my spare time sitting in a rocking chair and sipping weak tea. Sometimes I go really wild and rock back a little too far, but other than that . . ."

"Okay, okay. Make fun of me. And I guess pushing pills isn't a high-risk occupation."

"Well, there are those heavy sample cases. And most doctor's offices are probably filled with germs. Other than that, however, I think the job is about as safe as working in a health-food store."

He smiled, but she thought his eyes slid away from hers rather quickly. Was he hiding something? she wondered.

"How about your personal life?" she asked. "Ever been married, engaged, gone steady with the girl next door? You know almost everything about me and I know almost nothing about you."

He laughed and touched the scar on his cheek.

"Never married, never engaged. I've been tempted a few times, but it never worked out."

"Why not?"

"I guess my standards are as high as yours. I've always been looking for a woman who was a little different."

"And you think I might meet that criterion?" asked Summyr.

"I have my hopes."

"I may be different, but then so is the two-headed woman in the carnival."

He grinned. "Then you're lucky that I met you first."

Summyr laughed.

"You have a good honest laugh," said Steve. "Not one of those twitters that some women make like they're afraid to admit that something is really funny."

"You mean I sound like a hyena."

"But a very attractive female hyena."

It's been a long time since I've really laughed, Summyr thought. Probably since John died. She'd never turned into a twitterer, but in the last year she had usually let the smile die on her lips rather than have it blossom into a full laugh. It wasn't that she felt guilty enjoying things now that John was gone, but more that she was hesitant to fully participate in life for fear of what might happen.

"How did you get hooked up with selling pharmaceuticals?" she asked.

Steve shrugged. "I graduated from college and had no idea what I wanted to do. I'd majored in psychology, but I didn't want to go on to graduate school, at least not right away. I did different types of sales jobs for a few years, then I got into this."

"Think you'll stick with it?"

"Oh, definitely. I'm a very stable guy, you know. S-t-a-b-l-e," he spelled.

"Very funny," Summyr said, trying to look offended, but she found herself starting to smile. "There's one other thing I look for."

"What's that?"

"Honesty. If people care about each other, they should tell each other the truth. There shouldn't be any games."

Steve nodded.

"Do you agree with me?" Summyr prodded.

"Yes. The truth is always important," Steve said quickly, then turned his attention back to the view.

Chapter Five

"He's gorgeous," Chrissy said when Summyr returned after lunch, only about ten minutes late. "He has great hair and wonderful teeth."

"You make him sound like a winner in the Kentucky Derby," Summyr said.

"And he's taller than you are. The two of you make a great-looking couple."

Summyr had always worn flats when going out with John. They were the same height, and she felt awkward towering over him. It brought back all of her adolescent fears about being conspicuous. That would never happen with Steve. Summyr instantly dismissed the thought as incredibly shallow.

"There's more to picking a man than looks," she replied, sounding preachy even to herself.

"I suppose," Chrissy said in a slightly hurt tone.

"Look," she said more gently, "what I mean is that I hardly know Steve. We only met yesterday. He's a pretty good-looking guy, but I really don't know him well enough to decide if he's someone I want to get serious about."

"Then you should see him some more," Chrissy said. "You'll do that, won't you?"

"If he asks me, I might."

She heard Chrissy take in a breath, and waited for the inevitable lecture about getting on with her life and not dwelling on the past. But Chrissy remained silent. Feeling a rush of affection for such a good friend, Summyr gave her a hug.

"What's that for?" Chrissy asked, a smile of delight passing over her face.

"For being a great friend, and for letting me have an extra ten minutes for lunch."

Chrissy grinned and pushed several strands of hair out of her eyes. "If he had asked *me* to lunch, I wouldn't have been back again until the next morning," she said with such enthusiasm that Summyr had to laugh.

That night her yoga class was larger than usual. The evening classes usually drew around ten people, but tonight there were twelve. Three of them were new people, so Summyr made a point of doing a number of the basic postures and carefully demonstrating the right positioning of the hands and feet and how to focus your vision. *Drishti*, or gazing, points were very important, particularly when trying to do balancing postures such as the "dancer" or the "tree."

Alicia Molloy was there, and as usual doing everything to near perfection. At the end of class, Summyr stayed behind in the yoga studio, demonstrating several postures for the newcomers. When she was done and everyone had left, Summyr straightened the blankets and pillows into neat piles so everything would be ready for the next morning. As she walked out of the studio and into the lobby, she was surprised to see Alicia standing by her desk.

"Hi, can I help you?" she asked.

Alicia waved a check in her direction. "I wanted to pay for next month, but I didn't know where to put this."

Summyr took the check and put it in the wooden box on her desk. She always told students just to put the money or check in the box, then sign in, writing down how much they had paid. Summyr dedicated one afternoon a week to sorting out the paperwork and keeping the accounts straight. She was a little surprised that Alicia hadn't figured out the system with the box after a month of classes.

"You've had some yoga before?" Summyr asked, as Alicia sat down to put on her shoes.

"Sort of. I studied dance in college and did yoga exercises as part of that."

"A dancer. Well that explains why you're so flexible and graceful."

Alicia ignored the compliment. "I never did it professionally. I had to go to work and earn some money."

Summyr thought she detected a note of bitterness. She could well understand how a young woman might resent not being able to develop her talent. Summyr turned off the lights in the studio and took her coat off the coat tree behind her desk. She pulled her keys out of her pocket.

"We may as well go down together."

Alicia waited on the landing of the stairs, while Summyr locked the door to the studio behind her. Then they went down the stairs together into the warehouse. A single light glowed by the door to the outside, which was about thirty feet away from the foot of the stairs.

"It seems funny to see a warehouse so quiet and empty," Alicia suddenly said.

"I suppose you're right. If the owners have their way, I guess it won't be this way for long."

"What do you mean?"

"They plan to renovate the entire building, so I'm sure they aren't going to let this warehouse sit here as an empty space. Maybe they'll fix it up for offices."

"Are they going to do the same thing upstairs?"

Summyr realized that she hadn't really intended to announce her move to the students quite so soon. She had hoped to be able to give the address of her new location at the same time. Continuity was important in running any kind of business.

"Yes. That's the plan."

"So you'll be moving out." Alicia sounded so distressed that Summyr rushed to reassure her.

"I'm sure that I'll find another location quickly."

"When do you have to leave?"

"By the end of the month."

"Three and a half weeks," Alicia said, almost to herself.

"Like I said. I'll find another studio long before that. And there isn't much to move. Pillows, blankets, a few chairs, that's about all. My desk is the largest thing."

Summyr paused when she remembered John and herself moving the desk up the stairs on a spring day two years ago. That had been a very happy time, both of them filled with enthusiasm for her new business and their budding relationship. She felt tears sting the back of her eyes as she locked the outside door to the warehouse. The pain was so intense that Summyr leaned against the doorframe to catch her breath.

After a moment she turned around, hoping that Alicia hadn't noticed the moment of weakness, but she needn't have worried. Alicia had already walked across the parking lot without a word of good-bye and was getting into her car.

The heck with her, then, Summyr thought to herself. Little Miss Me-Me-Me. I hope my new yoga studio is real inconvenient for you. Summyr watched the woman pull out into the street. A car that had been parked across the way made a U-turn and headed in the same direction. The lights blinded Summyr for a moment and made her eyes water even more.

She gave herself a shake. Enough of this pathetic

behavior; time to get a grip. There are things to be done.

As she drove home, Summyr noticed that a light was on in her uncle's office. Feeling a sudden longing for a familiar face, she pulled in at the curb and parked. She rang the doorbell and stood directly in front of the peephole in the door, so her uncle would have no doubt as to who it was.

The door opened wide, and her uncle stood on the doorstep blinking at her in surprise.

"Is there anything wrong?"

"No," Summyr said, suddenly feeling that this had been a mistake. "I saw that your light was on and thought I'd drop by. Are you busy working on something? I'll go. I don't want to disturb you."

Her uncle opened the door wide and motioned for her to come in.

"My practice isn't so active that I have to work at night."

Summyr heard the strains of classical music coming from his office. Going into the room, she saw a book was lying facedown on the seat of one of the wingback chairs in front of the fireplace. The spine said that it was the poems of Elizabeth Barrett Browning. Her uncle saw her glance at the title.

"I'm afraid your uncle is an old romantic," he said with a sad smile, "but you already knew that."

Summyr sat in of the wingback chair and faced her uncle.

"You still miss her a great deal, don't you?" she asked.

He spread his hands as if to indicate that the answer was so obvious it didn't need to be spoken.

"The pain isn't as fresh as it was five years ago. But like a man who's lost an arm—the pain may disappear, but whenever he tries to reach for something he becomes aware of what he's lost all over again. The act of living makes me aware of how much I miss your mother."

"I'm sure my father misses her as well," Summyr said, feeling an obligation to defend him.

"I'm sure he does. But Sam was always in love with life as much as he was in love with Miriam. Now that she's gone, he's still got his other love."

Her uncle's implication that he had nothing left struck Summyr as sad but also as unhealthy. She'd heard the story many times while growing up—how Sam and her Uncle Harold had met Miriam at a dance. Harold was a twenty-year-old college student, while Sam was eighteen and just beginning to earn his living as a musician. Sam's group was performing at the dance, and Harold had promised to come along to hear them.

The petite laughing girl with the dark hair had immediately caught Harold's attention, and he had asked her to dance. They had danced three times in a row when Sam took a break and came down onto the dance floor to see his brother. Then, so quickly that Harold never knew how it happened, Sam and Miriam were talking about music. She had done some singing in high school and had always wanted to try out with a group.

"Why not right now?" Sam had said, pointing to the stage, his smile daring her to make good on her own ambitions.

Surprised at first, Miriam had quickly recovered, and after the break she was up on the stage belting out a song with more power than her tiny body would lead you to expect. And, as Harold had once told Summyr, that was how he saw Miriam for the rest of her life, on a stage above him with Sam at her side.

Sometimes the story touched her; sometimes it annoyed her. Loving someone deeply was one thing, but it was another thing to refuse to accept the inevitable and get on with your life. Harold had always been an attractive, successful man, and yet he had lived his life as if that one moment on a dance floor over thirty-five years ago had irrevocably set the course of his future.

"But I'm sure you understand how I feel. After all, you've lost someone whom you loved very deeply."

She didn't nod, not wanting to give any sign of agreeing that her grief was as obsessive as his.

"What was John like?" Summyr asked.

Her uncle glanced at her in surprise. "Surely you can answer that far better than I can."

"I'm not sure that I can remember things all that clearly anymore. I'm afraid that what I can recall of John is filtered through too many of my own imaginings and needs. Maybe I was actually too close to him. You knew him more as a colleague and a friend. What impressed you most about him?"

Harold stared into the empty fireplace for a long moment.

"He was fun."

The word 'fun' sounded so strange coming from Uncle Harold's lips that Summyr almost laughed.

"He had a marvelous sense of humor," her uncle continued. "Not a trait for which accountants are universally known, and he seemed to have such a great enthusiasm for life. There were times when he actually had me wishing that I were young again."

"I'm not sure that I would have thought of that as one of his qualities," Summyr said.

"That's very odd. One of clearest remembrances I have is of you laughing uproariously in the law library the first time that you met. It was the first that I had heard you laugh since your mother died, so I knew that John was good for you. Unfortunately . . ."

"Unfortunately, he wanted to risk his life with rock climbing," Summyr said bitterly.

Her uncle nodded. "True. But if John hadn't wanted to do that, then he wouldn't have been John."

"And if Miriam hadn't wanted to sing, she wouldn't have been Miriam," Summyr shot back.

They stared at each other in shocked surprise, like two people who had accidentally bumped heads while reaching for the same thing.

"Would you like a cup of tea?" her uncle asked, looking away. "It's decaffeinated."

"Thank you. That would be nice," Summyr replied.

Chapter Six

Summyr parked her car in front of the warehouse. With the morning paper folded open to the rental properties page under one arm, and her gym bag in the other hand, Summyr was awkwardly fumbling to get her key to the warehouse door out of her jacket pocket.

"Would you like a hand?"

Steve had suddenly materialized at her side. He was dressed all in black: black shorts, tight black T-shirt, and a black nylon windbreaker. More than ever he looked like a pirate . . . or a thief.

She handed Steve her gym bag and got her key out.

"You're bright and early this morning. Class doesn't start until ten."

He smiled. "Thought I'd come by to talk a little. But if you're busy . . ."

Summyr shook her head. She had planned to call

about a couple of rental properties listed in the morning paper, but that could always wait until after class.

"Come on up," she said, reaching out with the key
to unlock the warehouse door. As she started to push
the key into the lock, the door moved inward.

"That's funny. The door is open."

"Are there any other tenants who use the building?"
Steve asked.

She shook her head.

Gently but firmly, he moved her out of the doorway.

"You wait here, I'll go in and see what's going on."

"Shouldn't we call the police?"

"No sense bothering them until we're sure that
something's wrong," Steve said, giving her a wink and
disappearing inside.

Summyr waited outside for a few seconds, then she
took a tentative step inside the warehouse. The industrial ceiling lights had been turned on, which made her
feel better. Only someone who knew where the circuit
box was could have put on the power downstairs, so
perhaps the intruder was authorized. And what kind of
thief would put on the lights? Of course, with only
two small windows in the back that looked out on the
abandoned loading dock and a vacant lot, a brazen
robber might take a chance. But breaking into an
empty warehouse with a yoga studio above hardly
seemed worth the effort, unless he planned to steal
blankets and pillows.

As she thought these things, Summyr found herself
moving further inside the warehouse. She stopped to
listen but didn't hear any voices. There was a strange

smell in the air. The pungent aroma of smoke. She headed down the aisle between the empty shelves. Suddenly she heard a shout and the sound of raised voices coming from the far corner. Deciding that she'd be of more help to Steve on the scene than timidly waiting outside, Summyr began to walk quickly in the direction of the sound.

As she reached the back wall and turned the corner, she almost bumped into two men.

Steve was standing on the balls of his feet as though ready to pounce, his eyes fixed on a short fat man who was waving a cigar around and looking aggrieved.

"I told you, buddy, the owner sent me over here to look things over. I'm Louie Schuster. I've got a bid in to be the general contractor on this job."

"What job?" Steve asked.

"We're gonna renovate this whole building. Turn it into a real nice office space."

"I did get a notice to vacate the building by the end of the month," Summyr said.

Steve shot her a quick glance, then seemed to relax.

"Okay," he said, "but you should have notified the tenant that you were going to do an inspection."

"Yeah, well I didn't plan to go upstairs today. I was just checking out the warehouse area. That's unoccupied."

"When you do plan to look upstairs, make sure you notify Ms. Fox first," Steve said.

The sound of authority in his tone didn't seem to impress the contractor.

"Yeah, sure. He looked at his clipboard and read,

"Centered Self Yoga Studio." He puffed on his cigar, filling the air with smoke as though expressing his opinion on yoga. "Is that you?" he asked Summyr.

She nodded.

He gave her an appraising look. "I'll bet you're real flexible," he said with a grin.

"And be careful what you do with that cigar," Steve said. "If there's a fire in here, we'll know where to look."

"Don't worry about it," the man said, starting to turn his back on them.

Steve reached out and put a hand on the man's shoulder. He squeezed hard enough to get his attention.

"I'm not worried, but you should be. Give me or Ms. Fox a hard time, and the building inspector will be taking a particularly close look at everything you do here."

The fat man pulled away. He was clearly angry, but Summyr thought she caught a hint of concern in his eyes.

"Yeah, I'm careful. I've got a reputation to worry about."

"I'll bet you do," Steve said with a humorless smile.

"Why didn't you tell me about having to move?" Steve asked her as they went up the stairs to the studio.

"I haven't announced it to my classes yet. I've been hoping to have a new location all set up before making the information public."

Steve grinned. "And it wasn't really any of my business anyway, was it? Sorry."

"That's okay."

"It's just that I've only begun my yoga therapy, I'd hate to have to stop because you moved to a new location. Of course, maybe you give private lessons."

She tried to read his expression. He kept a straight face, but she thought she detected a hint of mischief in his eyes.

"Sometimes I do," she replied neutrally. "But we won't have to resort to that. I don't plan to move very far away because I've got lots of students who live in the area. I'm looking to find another place in town."

She went behind her desk and sat down—a good way to maintain some professional distance. Summyr still wasn't sure what to make of this guy. He was handsome, funny, and smart, but there was a hint of something a little bit dangerous about him. And danger was definitely something she'd had enough of in her last relationship. Steve sat on one of the chairs and began to take off his shoes.

"This business means a lot to you, doesn't it?"

Summyr nodded. "I've had other jobs since I've been out of school, but this is the first one where I've felt that I could really help people. Besides, yoga is more than just a job; it's really a way of life."

Steve smiled. "You mean the tofu and bean sprouts."

"Diet is part of it, although, as I told you yesterday, I'm not a true vegetarian."

"I remember. You can be tempted by the occasional steak."

"If it's with the right person," she said without

thinking, then realized that sounded awfully coy. "Anyway, the important thing about diet is that you not think about food all the time. Anything that distracts you from living in the moment, whether it be thinking about the past, wondering about the future, or wishing you had something you don't have, causes unhappiness."

"It must be hard to live up to that philosophy when you're worrying about where to rent next."

Summyr nodded. "Sometimes I lose my focus. But, after all, yoga is something you practice for a lifetime, not something you accomplish all at once."

He was staring at her with a particularly serious expression.

"You probably think I'm crazy," she said with an embarrassed laugh.

"No, actually I was just thinking how rare it is to find someone who thinks about things as deeply as you do."

"Is that a good thing?"

He laughed. "It certainly is a nice change from the folks who can only talk about their audio equipment, or where they're going on their next vacation, or the new car they just bought."

Summyr thought about her six-year-old car, her ancient CD player, and the fact that she hadn't had a real vacation in three years.

"Sometimes that stuff can be nice, too," she admitted. "But you shouldn't make it the center of your life."

"Yeah, things are nice, but it's what you do that makes life worthwhile."

He reached up with his right arm to hang his jacket on the wall and grimaced.

"Still hurts you quite a bit?" Summyr asked.

Steve tried to smile. "Only when I do certain things. I told the doctor and he said to me—just like the punch line of the old joke—if it hurts you, then don't do it."

"How much of your range of motion does he expect you to get back?"

He shrugged. "He's not sure. As I'm finding out more and more, medicine is not an exact science. It seems to depend on the individual patient. But one physical therapist in an accidental moment of complete truthfulness said that it might not be more than seventy-five percent. That means I may never be able to raise my right arm over my head."

Steve looked so sad when he said this that Summyr found herself wanting to go over and give him a hug, but she decided that her sympathy should take a more practical form.

"Would you hold your arms out in front of you with the palms down?" she asked.

Steve did as requested.

Summyr walked around the desk and stood behind him checking to see that his shoulder blades were even. The right one seemed a bit further back than the left, so she placed her hand on it and gently pushed forward.

"Tell me if I'm hurting you."

"That feels great."

"How long ago was your surgery?"

"Two months."

"What did the therapist have you do for rehab?"

"Mostly exercises with elastic bands to help strengthen the shoulder and increase mobility."

"Did you do them?" she asked with a smile.

"You bet. I take that kind of thing seriously," Steve replied.

"It's just that lots of people think that the surgery will cure everything, so they don't have to make any effort afterwards."

"I played some football in high school and college, and I guess I've still got the athlete's mind-set when it comes to exercise. I think it's important."

Summyr nodded and walked around to stand in front of Steve, who was still managing to hold his hands out in front. She reached out and grasped both his hands, then gently drew him toward her, exerting equal pull on both arms.

"Try to resist my pulling," she said.

After a moment she saw him flinch.

"Pain?"

He nodded. "In the back of my right shoulder."

"Try to hang on for half a minute more."

"Did you learn this from yoga?"

"When I started getting students who had injuries, I went over to the hospital and spent several hours a day for a couple of months going around with the therapists to see the kinds of things they did. That's why they send post-op patients to me. They know I'm not going to do them any harm."

"That's reassuring," Steve said through clenched teeth.

"Okay," Summyr said, releasing his hands. "You can relax now."

Instead of dropping his arms, Steve took a step forward and wrapped his arms around her. Startled, Summyr stood there with her arms at her side, then she found herself returning his hug.

"You know," Steve whispered in her ear, "this helps stretch the shoulder joints, too, and it's a lot more pleasant."

"I don't think this is an approved therapy exercise."

"Well, it should be. It's good for the body and for the soul," he murmered.

Summyr pressed closer to him, feeling the warmth of his body through the thin cotton of her T-shirt. How nice to lose myself in this kind of closeness with somebody again, she thought.

Someone cleared her throat from the direction of the doorway. Summyr opened her eyes and saw Mrs. Benson standing there with a wide smile on her face.

"Oh, goody, team yoga today. I hope you brought a partner for me."

Summyr and Steve separated.

"We were just . . ." Summyr began.

"I know what you were doing. I'm not *that* old," the woman said. "And you make a fine-looking couple, if I do say so."

Steve smiled at Summyr.

"That's what I think, but I'm not sure that she's convinced."

"Well, it looks to me like you're taking the right steps to convince her. Sometimes a little action is more persuasive than lots of talk," Janet said.

Summyr looked at the clock and saw that class was due to start in fifteen minutes. Quickly slipping off her shoes, she went into the studio and turned on the lights and the relaxing music she played before class. She tried to focus her mind on the moment, but her thoughts were bouncing around like Mexican jumping beans. When she had prepared the studio for class, and Steve, Mrs. Benson, and two college students were seated, Summyr sat in the half-lotus position, closed her eyes, and tried to clear away all thoughts.

She tried to push away the image of Steve and how it had felt to be in his arms. She slid her thoughts away from any comparison between the way she had just felt, and how it had been when she was held by John. She tried not to focus on the fact that she had to tell the class today that the studio had to move. Since two people knew already, it really wasn't fair to others to keep it secret. By concentrating on her breath, the pictures in her head gradually disappeared, and she felt a sense of serenity take their place.

When she finally opened her eyes she was centered and ready to begin the class. Just then Alicia came in and walked quickly but gracefully across the center of the room. Summyr watched as Steve's eyes carefully followed her every movement.

Suddenly all of her serenity disappeared.

Chapter Seven

"What did they say when you told them about having to move?" Chrissy asked.

"There were only five people there, and Alicia and Steve already knew. But Janet Benson's reaction made up for both of them. She shouted, 'You aren't going to close, are you?' so loudly that we all jumped. I tried to reassure her that I'd find a new place before we had to leave, but I don't think she was convinced."

"I'm not surprised that she'd be worried. When I saw her in the store last night, she was telling me how much she's benefited from yoga. Her back is better than it has been for years, and she thinks that she's gotten a lot stronger in general. She's a walking advertisement for you."

"That's good to hear." So Janet came back again last night after visiting me in the store in the morning to talk about Chrissy, Summyr thought. I wonder if she's already got her "Change Chrissy" project under way. "Was she here for something in particular?"

"Kava tea. She said you gave her some. After that we talked for a while."

The way Chrissy nervously bobbed her head told Summyr that the conversation had been disturbing in some way.

Summyr busied herself rearranging the advertising pamphlets on the counter.

"What did you talk about?" she asked with forced casualness.

At first she didn't think Chrissy was going to answer because her face remained turned toward the computer screen, as if the inventory list was a pressing matter.

"She said that I should be making more of myself," Chrissy finally said in an almost inaudible voice.

Summyr warned herself not to chime in with her own endorsement of that opinion too readily.

"I see. I wonder what she meant by that."

"She said that I was a smart, organized young woman, and I was wasting myself in a place where the manager didn't appreciate me and the absentee owners were only concerned with the bottom line."

Janet certainly pulled out all the stops, Summyr thought.

"What did you say?"

Chrissy turned to face her and her voice rose.

"I told her that she was wrong about Richie, that he does realize all that I do around here. And that I've been interested in organic foods for years, so that's the kind of store where I want to work. I'm not interested in being tied down in some office job where I have twenty people over me telling me what to do. Here at least I'm pretty much my own boss."

Summyr had to admit to herself that Richie's laziness did have that one good effect.

"What did Janet say to all that?"

Chrissy grinned sheepishly. "I think I scared her a little. I guess I was almost shouting. She apologized for sounding like she was telling me what to do. After that I calmed down and we had a good talk. She really is a nice lady."

Summyr agreed and let a moment of silence pass.

"You know she might have one point."

"What's that?" Chrissy asked suspiciously.

"The part about this being kind of a dead-end job. I mean there really isn't much chance of promotion."

"Yeah, that's true. But you do understand what I said about being my own boss, right? I mean, after all, you could be out making lots of money if you didn't have the yoga center. Still, that's what you want to do, so you do it."

"You've got a point there," Summyr said, realizing that her own position on this whole matter was none too strong. "All I'm suggesting is that with your managerial experience you might find a store similar to this where you might have more opportunities."

Chrissy put her hands on her hips and faced Summyr. "There are two organic food stores in town. One is run by a national chain, and there's this one. The only way I could do something like you're talking about is to set up my own store, and I don't have the kind of capital to do that. It isn't like owning your own yoga studio where all you have to shell out for are a dozen blankets and pillows. A place like this has tens of thousands of dollars in inventory."

"Sounds like you've given it some thought," said Summyr.

"I'm not as unambitious as I look," Chrissy said, suddenly angry.

Summyr put her hand on her friend's arm. "I know you're not. And you have the ability to do anything you want to do."

"Tell my mother that. Whenever I mention some new idea I have for increasing sales here, she says, 'Why bother, Chrissy, it isn't your store. Leave the thinking to the people at the top.' And, you know, some days I think she's right. Why try so hard when no one cares? And it really isn't my store, even though I fool myself into thinking it is sometimes."

Chrissy pulled strands of hair out of her face, which had gotten bright red as she talked.

"I see what you're saying," said Summyr softly. "You've got your mother telling you not to make any effort, and Janet is pushing you to do more."

"Yeah. And I know that in a way Janet is right, but I don't really see how to take the next step."

"I know what you mean. I spent the hour before I came in here calling on rental ads in the newspaper for business space."

"Any luck?" Chrissy asked, calming down now that she was no longer the topic of conversation.

"Most of them are divided up into office spaces without a large enough open area for a yoga studio. The realtors said that I could pay to have interior walls taken down as long as they weren't load bearing, but I couldn't even afford the rent at a place that would have enough square footage for a studio. You can't do yoga in a closet."

"Yeah, it's the same thing with dance. Do you remember Cheryl Roth?"

"She had that dance school?"

Chrissy nodded. "She had her school in that building in the center of town, the one that's for sale now. The landlord kept raising the rent until finally she had to move out."

"Where is she teaching now?"

"She went in with someone else who had their own building on the south end."

"Maybe her old space is still available."

"It probably is, but I doubt that you could afford that place either. I seem to remember that it was about half again what you're paying now. And since the landlord is trying to sell the building, he hasn't been keeping up with the maintenance. It could need a lot of work."

"Too bad. A former dance studio would be an ideal spot, and that building backs on public parking. It would be pretty handy. I think I'll give a call on it anyway when I get a chance. Maybe the landlord is tired of having it empty and might come down on the rent."

"So how are you and the handsome Steve getting along?" Chrissy asked, giving Summyr a mischievous smile.

"Okay," Summyr said.

"Come on. There must be more to say than that. Did he show up for class today?"

"Oh, yes. In fact he helped me deal with an intruder."

"An intruder!" Chrissy said, opening her eyes wide.

Summyr explained about the encounter with Louie Schuster.

"Sounds like a first-rate sleaze to me. It's a good thing Steve was there."

"I could have handled it fine myself," said Summyr, but she knew that having Steve by her side when confronting the contractor had made her feel more secure.

"So when are you two going out again?"

Summyr shrugged. She wasn't going to tell her friend that their yoga therapy had turned into a hugging session. Janet might tell Chrissy, Summyr couldn't help that, but she wasn't going to volunteer the information.

"Maybe we won't," she said.

"Why not?" Chrissy said, the disappointment evident in her voice.

"He hasn't asked me out."

Although she wasn't about to admit it to Chrissy, Summyr had been more than half-expecting Steve to say something after class about their going out again.

But giving her a quick wave, he had left after class, hot on the heels of Alicia. Watching out the window, Summyr had noticed that he didn't try to talk to Alicia, but he had carefully watched her get in her car, then pulled down the driveway behind her.

"You could ask him out," Chrissy said.

"Look, he seems interested in me when we're alone, but every time Alicia Molloy comes along he stares at her like she's honey and he's the bee."

"Oh." Chrissy stood silent for a moment, then her face brightened. "But, you know, Richie looks at other women all the time, and I don't let that discourage me."

Maybe you should, Summyr thought, but she didn't say anything. There was no point in hurting Chrissy's feelings; they were tender enough after her recent confrontation with Janet Benson.

"I've been thinking about John lately," Summyr said slowly.

Out of the corner of her eye she saw Chrissy's head come up from the papers she was checking over.

"You've thought about him a lot ever since he died," her friend said. "That's only natural."

Summyr gave Chrissy a gentle smile of appreciation at the attempt to comfort her.

"Actually, I've thought about him less and less as time has gone by. For the first couple of months, I felt like he was still here. I found myself talking to him as if he were right beside me. And most nights he appeared in my dreams."

"What was he doing?" Chrissy asked, fascinated.

"Usually something I'd seen him do hundreds of times. We might be sitting at a table drinking coffee, and I'd have this image of him looking at me over the top of his coffee cup the way he always did. Or he'd be behind the wheel of the car, and turn to listen to something I was saying. I'd think, 'Oh, John isn't dead after all.' But then, even though I was dreaming, I'd immediately know that wasn't true. It was like reliving his death all over again every night."

"That's terrible," Chrissy said.

Summyr nodded. "But now it hardly happens at all. Now I worry more about forgetting him. I can't bring his face to mind as quickly as I used to, and I'm starting to wonder if I really remember the way we were together."

"What do you mean?"

Summyr paused, not sure how much she wanted to reveal about last night's conversation with her uncle.

"My uncle told me yesterday that one of the things he remembers most about John is his sense of humor. How he made people laugh. That's not the way I remember John."

Chrissy hesitated. "Well," she finally began, "a sense of humor is a pretty subjective thing, but I remember John as being funny. Maybe not knee-slapping funny, but he had a dry sense of humor and never took things too seriously. That was one of the things that surprised me about him, because I'd always had this image of accountants as being kind of serious and stuffy, but John wasn't like that at all."

Summyr sighed. "I don't remember him as being

stuffy, either. But I think of him as being stable, as someone you could count on."

"He was that, too, Summyr. But a person can be funny and still be responsible."

"Does a responsible person go rock climbing when they're engaged to be married?"

Chrissy looked down at the counter, trying to compose an answer.

"Don't bother trying to answer that," Summyr said, smiling slightly. "It wasn't a fair question. Anyway, it's the one I should be asking myself, not you."

"I'm sure John never took any unnecessary risks. He talked about how he checked his equipment and made sure that he was in good shape. And you heard what the people climbing with him said: they had never seen a rock face shatter like that. There wasn't anything John could have done to avoid it."

"I know, I know. And he never hid from me that he rock climbed. I went out with him and got engaged to him fully aware that this was his hobby, and he wasn't about to give it up. Somehow it never bothered me until it got close to the wedding. I guess I always thought that once we actually married, he'd stop taking chances. But I was only fooling myself, and not being honest with him."

"I'm sure you'd have worked it out," Chrissy began, then stopped, horrified at where the statement was going.

"If we'd had more time," Summyr said with a grim smile. "I think you might be right. Maybe we both would have had to make some changes, but we'd have gotten through it. The sad thing is, now we'll never know."

Chrissy nodded. "Well, one good thing about Steve, aside from his being gorgeous, is that he doesn't do anything dangerous. I mean how risky is lugging around a bag of drug samples all day. And you said that he doesn't have any dangerous hobbies."

"That's true," Summyr said. She felt oddly disappointed at hearing Steve described as being so safe and sane. That wasn't the way it felt to be with him. There seemed to be something edgier and more exciting about him when he was actually sitting across the table.

"You don't sound very happy about Steve's conservative lifestyle."

"I guess I don't know what I want," Summyr said with a sigh. "I want security and excitement at the same time. I want a guy who takes chances, but doesn't take risks. I want someone who lives life to the fullest, but has plans to live to a ripe old age. I guess I just want it all."

"I think you've got a problem," said Chrissy.

"I think you're right."

Chapter Eight

"Well, this is it," Beryl announced, pushing open the door at the top of the stairs.

Summyr took a step inside. It was cavernous. The ceilings went up at least fifteen feet and the room itself she estimated to be seventy-five feet long and probably fifty feet wide. Aside from the supporting pillars at regular intervals there were no walls to impede visibility. One long wall was mirrored, so the dancers could watch their form, and a *barre* was still in place along a short wall for pre-dance warm-ups. Useful for stretching before yoga as well, Summyr thought.

"So what do you think?" Beryl asked. "Pretty amazing, isn't it?"

"Amazing is the word," Summyr said, walking across the hardwood floor to look out the one large window in the front of the building. Down below the town green was spread out in front of her like a post-card. She watched the traffic go around the circle, thinking how this location seemed to put you directly in touch with Eastfield. You could practically feel the rhythms of the New England town.

"And there's free public parking right in back," Beryl said as if reading her mind.

Beryl had gone to high school with her. So when Summyr decided to take a look at the former dance school the next morning, she'd contacted the real estate agency Beryl worked for, and they had gotten the key to the building.

"You said as we were coming over here that the landlord might consider lowering the rent?"

"Shh," Beryl said with a gleam in her eye, then she winked. "Remember, I'm supposed to be representing the owner. But to be honest, he's in trouble. Rumor has it that one of his businesses is deep in the red. He tried to raise the rent here to cover his losses, but the kind of people who rent in this part of town can't pay what he wants. Cheryl moved out and so did the guy who had the store downstairs. All he's got in here now is somebody in the office space on the Main Street side, but he's leaving at the end of the month."

"So now he's trying to sell the building?"

"Right. But he isn't having much luck there either. The building needs work."

Summyr took a second look around. The walls were rather dingy. The coat of cream paint was obviously many years old and had darkened to an off-yellow over time. The paint on the ceiling was peeling in spots and the sill under the large window was rotting away. Still, Summyr thought, beggars can't be choosers. If the rent was right she'd take it and worry about the other problems later. Live in the moment, after all, that was what she told her students. The hardwood floor, however, which had been ideal for the dancers would have to be covered with some sort of carpeting. Yoga postures, at least for westerners, required that there be some cushioning for the body. She wondered what it would cost to carpet even a fraction of this area.

"The real problems are with the mechanicals," Beryl continued. "I doubt that the plumbing and heating have been updated in the last fifty years. Plus he was asking way more than it was worth. But I've heard that he recently lowered the price. I guess he's getting desperate."

"So if I rented the place from him and then it sold, what would happen to me?" asked Summyr.

"It would depend on the terms of the lease. Have your uncle get you a long-term lease so that even if it sells, the new owner can't raise your rent for a few years. In fact, I would have your uncle handle the whole thing. This is a business transaction, so let him negotiate for you."

Summyr smiled to herself. Her uncle might be a giant teddy bear when it came to her, but she'd heard enough around town to know that he had a reputation as a tough and shrewd attorney.

"I think I'll call him this morning."

Downstairs she said good-bye to Beryl and thanked

her for all the help. As she walked back to her car, she passed the abandoned storefront. Summyr walked up to the dirty glass and peered inside. The room seemed to be very long and narrow. It looked as though the room had a tin ceiling, she thought as she walked to her car, quite an elegant touch. There was real potential for that space as well as for the upstairs.

She usually spent Thursday mornings at the yoga studio taking care of bills and checking up on student payments. Although most yoga students were honest, a few of them had a tendency to feel that money was not a matter that they should allow to cloud their consciousness. This meant that unless gently encouraged, some students would easily forget to pay for their classes. Summyr had developed a technique of approaching these individuals and saying that it was certainly a sign of their deepening contemplative practice which she was sorry to disturb, but unfortunately on this earthly plane, money had to be exchanged. Most responded without any difficulty.

As Summyr pulled into the parking lot by the warehouse, she was disturbed herself to see that once again the door to the warehouse stood open: an indication that Louis Schuster was inside. For a moment she considered driving away and leaving the paperwork for another day. But years of living in a family where her parents had depended on her to do a grown-up's chores from an early age had taught her not to flee from difficult situations, so she got out of her car and proceeded boldly to the warehouse door.

As she went inside, she was surprised to see that the lights in the warehouse bay weren't on the way they had been the other day. She switched on the lights for the stairway and went upstairs. When she reached the landing, the door to the yoga center stood partially open.

Schuster must be in the studio, Summyr thought angrily, he promised to give me some warning. Now here he is showing up without telling me.

She pushed the door open the rest of the way and went inside. Summyr went into the studio fully expecting to see the overweight contractor striding around on the carpet in muddy work boots. Instead, he was lying in the middle of the studio floor, flat on his back in the "corpse" pose, the one traditionally used for deep relaxation. For an instant Summyr thought with surprise that he must be practicing yoga, then she saw an overturned ladder and realized that something else must have happened. Quickly she rushed over to his side. That was when she saw the bloody gash on the side of his head. A metal toolbox was about a foot from where he lay, and Summyr surmised that he had fallen from the ladder and struck his head on the sharp edge.

She went back to her office, dialed 911, and asked the operator to send an ambulance. She got a cup of water from the cooler and returned to Schuster's side, where she used a tissue to gently clean the blood from his wound.

"What?" the contractor said, flinching awake as soon as she placed the cloth firmly on his head.

"What's going on?" He rolled away from her and tried to get to his feet, but then collapsed back on his side and clutched at his right leg.

"Don't try to get up, Mr. Schuster. You've had a fall," Summyr said.

He rolled on his back and glared up at her, his beady eyes bulging out from the folds of his pudgy face.

"What happened to me?" he demanded, managing to imply that it was somehow her fault.

"I have no idea," Summyr replied coolly. She was rapidly becoming less sympathetic to the man as he showed more signs of life and his hostile attitude reappeared.

"How did I fall?"

"I don't know."

He tried to get up again, then groaned and flopped back down.

"What a headache!" He reached up and touched his forehead. When he looked at his hand and saw blood, his eyes popped open even wider. "I'm hurt. Why are you just sitting there? I'm hurt."

"The ambulance is on the way." Summyr pushed the cup of water in his direction. "Would you like a drink?"

Reluctantly he took the cup. Summyr helped him up into a seated position and he took a sip of water. While she waited for him to get done drinking, Summyr noticed that a tile had been taken down from the ceiling right above the ladder.

"What were you doing up on the ladder?" she asked.

"Checking the ceiling," he replied, dribbling water

down his chin. "The new owner wanted me to see if it could be raised a few feet."

"What did you find out?"

Schuster gave her a what-business-is-it-of-yours look, then apparently decided that he might need Summyr's help in getting to his feet.

"The original ceiling is two feet above this one. We can rip these tiles out and expose the original one real easy."

"How did you fall?"

He shook his head, then groaned.

"I had my head up above the ceiling when all of a sudden the ladder started to twist under me. I tried to grab on the braces that hold the tiles in place, but before I could reach them I fell. That's all I remember."

Summyr looked over at the aluminum ladder. It looked like the one that she kept in the closet for changing lightbulbs.

"You used my ladder?"

"Yeah. I only had a wooden one on the truck and I wasn't going to bust a gut lugging that up all these stairs, not once I found yours. I should have known that a cheap thing like that wouldn't hold me."

"To get up as high as you did, you were probably beyond the top step that you're supposed to use, right?" asked Summyr. Not to mention that you're probably over the weight limit for a light aluminum ladder, Summyr thought.

Schuster didn't answer.

"Where's that ambulance, anyway?" he grumbled.

The sound of a siren pulling into the parking lot answered his question.

"I'll go downstairs and direct them up here," Summyr said.

She met the EMTs at the warehouse door and told them where to find Schuster, then she stayed downstairs in the warehouse. She didn't really want to talk to the contractor anymore or listen to what would no doubt be a litany of complaints as they tried to get him ready for transport. After about fifteen minutes, the two EMTs appeared at the top of the stairs and slowly began to bring the stretcher down the steep wooden steps. The strain of carrying the overweight man showed on their rapidly reddening faces.

"Can't you guys take it easy? I've got a heck of a headache here, and I think my leg is broken," Schuster whined.

One of the men carrying the stretcher gave Summyr a small smile of exasperation as they finally reached the warehouse level.

"And you," Schuster said, catching sight of Summyr. "I'll be talking to my attorney about suing you for that defective ladder."

Summyr felt her dislike of the man reach the boiling point.

"Good. Because I'll be having my lawyer get in touch with you about illegal trespass," she snapped back.

Schuster was about to respond when the stretcher bearer nearest his head gave that stretcher an abrupt shake.

"Watch what you're doing back there, sonny," the contractor bellowed.

"Sorry," the man said and gave Summyr a wink as they carried their burden out to the ambulance.

"Don't forget my toolbox," came Schuster's muffled voice from inside the ambulance, and the EMT who had shaken the stretcher ran back upstairs and retrieved it.

"If they were all nice, then it wouldn't be a job," he whispered to Summyr as he walked past.

"Does he really have a broken leg?"

"Looks like it."

Great, Summyr thought, the guy breaks a leg trespassing in my studio and using my ladder, and he threatens to sue *me*.

Once the ambulance left the parking lot, Summyr took the precaution of locking the downstairs door, then went up to the yoga center. Too keyed up to do paperwork, she hauled the vacuum cleaner out of its tiny closet and began cleaning the carpet. With all the use it got, she usually did it three times a week. When she came to the area where Schuster had fallen, Summyr folded up her ladder, noticing that the rails which held the sides of the ladder extended had been bent outward by Schuster's weight. It was still usable, but she'd have to be careful. It would be bound to wobble if she tried to go up very far.

She got down on her knees to look at the carpet in the area of the accident to check for any signs of blood. That would have to be cleaned up before the next class. In this day and age, it wouldn't be considered hygienic to have students exposed to blood. If she hadn't been studying the carpet so closely she probably would never have found the gold post for pierced ears, and it would have ended up in the vacuum. It was buried in the nap of the carpet as if it had fallen and then been stepped on. Probably Alicia's, Summyr thought. She usually put her mat in that spot for class, and she had been there only yesterday. I'll check with her tomorrow to see if it's hers.

Finished with the vacuuming, Summyr returned to her desk and quickly paid a few bills. She then carefully checked the past week's payments, and made a few notes as to who was overdue. It was only when she glanced out the window to rest her eyes for a moment that Summyr remembered that she had meant to call her uncle and have him check on the possibility of renting the former dance studio. Probably it wouldn't hurt to mention Schuster's accident either, just in case he really did try to proceed with his ridiculous lawsuit.

Mrs. Forbes, her uncle's secretary since as far back as Summyr could remember, put her through right away. When her uncle came on the line, he sounded different.

"Are you all right, Uncle Harold?" Summyr asked.

"Of course, who wouldn't be all right on a day as lovely as this one," he replied with such enthusiasm that Summyr looked out the window again to make sure that it was still as cloudy as it had been ten minutes ago.

"What's going on?" she asked suspiciously.

"What do you mean? Can't your old uncle be in a good mood for a change?"

"Not without a reason."

He paused.

"I am your only family north of Florida. So maybe you should tell me what's going on."

He cleared his throat as if about to embark on a major speech. "I just met a woman," he announced.

Summyr waited for more, but apparently her uncle was not going to share any further information without prompting. A woman! She might have expected the culmination of some important business deal or the appointment to some post in local government to have him giddy with joy. But a woman! That was certainly a change. He had gone out a few times over the years, but none of these relationships had ever amounted to anything serious.

"In Harold's mind, none of them will ever match Miriam," Summyr's father had always said, with a mixture of sadness and satisfaction, when he heard the report of another failed relationship. Her mother had just sighed. One of her great sorrows had been that Harold had never gotten over her. She frequently tried to convince Harold to move on with his life, but the more attention she paid to him, the more his devotion seemed to increase. Perhaps now that her mother was gone, Summyr thought, her uncle would be able to start over where he had left off on that dance floor over thirty-five years ago.

"How did you meet her?" Summyr asked.

"She came to me," he replied, his voice filled with

happy disbelief. "She wanted me to handle a real estate transaction for her. We started to talk about this and that, and before long I was asking her out."

"You asked her out?"

There was a long pause. "You know, I'm not sure. Somehow it just seemed that we agreed to go out together tonight."

Suddenly Summyr felt rather concerned. Her uncle was a successful and well-respected man, she didn't want him falling into the hands of some woman who was only out for his money.

"Do you know anything about this woman?"

"I know she's a widow of about my age and has enough money to buy a major piece of real estate in town. Other than that, all I know is that she moved to town recently from Connecticut. I expect that I'll learn more tonight."

"Well," Summyr said doubtfully.

"Don't worry about me, Summyr. I'm not going to fall into the clutches of some gold digger. I've spent years keeping women at bay, I'm not likely to change overnight." He paused for a moment, then said in a slightly accusing tone, "You should be happy for me."

"I am," Summyr replied, trying to match his enthusiasm. "I think it's really great. I hope it works out for you."

"We'll just have to see," her uncle said, with more pleasure in his voice than the cautious words would indicate. "Now I'm sure you didn't call because you had some intuition that I had finally gotten a date."

Summyr first explained about the incident with Schuster.

"Well, the landlord certainly does have a right to reasonable access to the premises, but I would bet that your lease requires him to give you at least twenty-four hours notice. Was there any message on your answering machine telling you he was coming?"

"No."

"I'll look at your lease, but I suspect that he shouldn't have been there, nor, under any circumstances, should he have used your ladder."

"So I'm in the clear?"

"No attorney will ever guarantee you that," her uncle said with a brief chuckle, "but I think that Schuster was just shooting his mouth off because his head hurt. I doubt very much that he'll actually attempt to sue. Also, he's got a local business; he won't want to get a reputation as a troublemaker."

"Okay. Now there's something else I wanted to ask you about," Summyr began, and she described her visit to the former dance studio. "I know that the place is for sale, but I'm wondering if I couldn't rent there anyway, at least until a new owner takes over and decides to renovate."

There was a long pause on the other end of the line. "Uncle Harold?"

"I'm sorry Summyr, but I'm afraid that what was happy news to me is going to be disappointing news for you. The woman I was telling you about has just made an offer on that building. The deal hasn't closed yet, but I think the current landlord will accept it. The building has been on the market for quite a while."

Summyr groaned.

"She plans to fix the building up very nicely."

"But then I won't be able to afford to rent there." Summyr paused and decided there was no sense in spoiling her uncle's happy mood. "Well, I'm sure that something will turn up for me."

"I'll keep looking," Uncle Harold promised.

After thanking her uncle, Summyr hung up and stared across the room. Things were definitely not going well. In three weeks she had to have a new space to move into. Nothing in the paper that met her needs had been within her price range. She'd even had Beryl do a computer search of available business rentals and that had come up empty as well. Her yoga master, Ananda, had often told her to listen to the universe and try to hear what it was telling you. Too many people try to change the universe, he warned, instead of listening to the universe and adjusting. It is far easier to move with the wind than against it.

So what is the universe trying to tell me, that I should give up my yoga studio and get an office job? Summyr thought. Well, if that's what it's saying, the universe is going to have to speak a lot louder before I go along with it.

Chapter Nine

"Okay, now everyone find a *drishti*, that's a gazing point, and focus on it. That way you'll be able to maintain your balance," Summyr told the class, then she slowly led them into the "tree" posture where they stood on one foot and extended their arms over their heads.

She looked around the room and saw ten pairs of arms stretched toward the ceiling. Several people had to lower their raised foot to the floor as they began to lose balance. Summyr always told people that it was okay to lower the foot, regain balance, then go back to the balancing posture. The important thing was to be in harmony with your body and not feel the need to meet some external standard based on what other members of the class were able to do.

Good thing they aren't comparing themselves to Alicia, Summyr thought. The woman stood there straight and steady, her blue eyes unwavering and her standing leg giving the impression that it could hold her body all night if necessary. It had been a surprise to see Alicia at an evening class; she usually came only to the morning classes. When Summyr had shown her the earring, she had allowed that it might be hers and that she had lost one recently. She had seemed reluctant to take it, as if someone else might accuse her of being a thief. Finally, Summyr had suggested that she take it home and compare it to the remaining one to see if they were a match.

Bringing them down from the "tree," Summyr immediately led them into a "half moon" pose. She went around the room and gently straightened several of the newer students who had bent forward from the waist instead of staying in a straight plane. Yoga wasn't just a matter of stretching in a precise way. To do the postures carefully, mindfully, as yoga masters liked to say, was a way to discipline the mind as well as the body.

Ten students was a respectable class. If only she could offer more evening classes. Who am I kidding, Summyr thought, feeling her own peace of mind skitter away, I'll be lucky if I'm offering any classes at all once the end of the month comes around. She took a cleansing breath and felt her heartbeat gradually slow. No sense stressing about the future, all she could do is act with intelligence and hope things worked out. Worry would only get in the way of intelligent action.

When the class ended Summyr spent some time

chatting with students, showed a new student how to do the "child" pose correctly, then removed the night's payment from the box and locked the money in her desk. It was hardly enough to justify a thief's effort, but there was no sense in leaving things around, especially now when Schuster might come prowling around at any time.

After turning down the heat and putting out the lights, Summyr slipped into her green nylon jacket. Going out on the landing she carefully locked the door behind her, then stood for a moment looking down at the warehouse. With only the one light above the stairway, most of it was lost in shadows. Although darkness usually didn't bother her, there was something that struck her as not quite right. Summyr couldn't put her finger on it, so she stood for a moment breathing softly, trying to sense what it was that had disturbed her.

She went down the stairs and switched on the lights for the warehouse floor. With Schuster coming around on his so-called inspection tours, she decided it might be prudent to see if he had been getting up to anything. She walked up and down the aisles of empty shelves, not seeing anything out of the ordinary until she turned down the last aisle. A cool breeze struck her face.

When Summyr reached the back wall, she saw that the window had been left open. In all the time she had rented there, Summyr had never seen one of these windows open. In fact, she hadn't been certain that they even could be opened since the frames were crusted over with dirt and paint. Probably more of Schuster's doing, thought Summyr, the man was definitely a menace. She went to the window and looked outside. The opening was only about five feet above the loading dock, offering easy access to the inside. With only a vacant field behind the building, having the window open was definitely a security hazard. She carefully closed and locked it. The last thing she needed was for some kids or a homeless person to get inside and start a fire.

When Summyr reached the door to the warehouse to lock up, she paused again to see if things felt right to her now. Amazing how I noticed that, she thought, maybe there is something to all this talk about listening to the universe.

As soon as Summyr reached Root and Branch the next morning, she knew that something was going on. It wasn't the voice of the universe, but raised human voices coming from the middle of the store.

"I think we should move all the weight reduction items up to the front of the store," a woman was saying firmly in harsh nasal tones.

Summyr went in search of the voice. At the end of the third aisle, Richie and Chrissy were listening to an extremely thin woman with perfectly coiffed blond hair, who was wearing a professional-looking pin-striped suit.

"Weight reduction products will increase our appeal to younger women."

Richie nodded vigorously. "Excellent idea, Andrea, it's always good to get that younger demographic."

"Most women who come in are looking for something to relieve stress, not increase it," Chrissy said. She looked sullen and her hair was hanging down like a curtain, half-covering her face.

"Hello," Summyr said.

"Hey, Kiddo," Richie said. "I'd like you to meet Andrea, a friend of mine."

He threw an arm around the blond woman as if to guarantee that there was no misunderstanding that friend meant girlfriend. In her high heels she was as tall as he was.

Summyr smiled at the woman who studiously ignored her, staring intently at the items on the shelves.

"And why don't you have sale items on the end caps where people can find them?" she asked, pointing at the shelf with a one-inch-long enameled nail.

"Why is that?" Richie repeated, looking accusingly at Chrissy.

"Because we send out a monthly brochure with all the sale items listed, and you said that we should put the sales at the back of the store so people had to walk past everything else to find them. *You* thought it would increase impulse buying."

He stared at Chrissy with an expression of betrayal.

"Well, perhaps I was wrong on that one." He turned to Summyr. "Andrea works in a department store, so I asked her to come in and look over the way we display our sales merchandise."

"Well, I suppose there are a lot of similarities between a health-food store and a department store," Summyr said, struggling to keep the sarcasm out of her voice.

Andrea's pale blue eyes, placed on either side of a long pinched nose, focused on Summyr, as if to warn her that Richie might be stupid, but she knew an insult when she heard one.

"Sales are sales," Richie said blithely. "If you can sell perfume, you can sell cement. It's all the same."

Obviously another saying from his one course at community college, Summyr conjectured.

"And the whole store is far too cluttered," Andrea concluded, waving a limp hand in a sweeping gesture that included the surrounding universe.

"People come in looking for specific products," Chrissy replied, her lips starting to quiver. "We have to be able to provide them."

"Have you ever heard of individual ordering?" Andrea asked with a patronizing smile. "You make the customer pay for the product, then you order it for them. Once the customer orders the product, then you're assured of a sale. That way you can keep down inventory."

"Many of our suppliers are small, and it can take them weeks to send us a product. Our customers will go to the other organic store in town if we don't have it on the shelf," Chrissy replied.

"So we lose a few customers, in the long run it will increase profits," Andrea replied.

"We can't afford to lose *any* customers," Chrissy snapped.

"Now, now," Richie said, flashing a big smile at Chrissy. "We all get a little defensive when someone questions the way we've been doing things. But we have to be willing to change. Remember, to change is to grow."

Chrissy pulled her hair out of her face and glared at Andrea's back as the blond woman drifted off toward the refrigerator area at the back of the store, continuing her inspection tour.

"In fact," Richie continued, "I've been thinking that it might be a good idea if we brought in a real professional like Andrea to take over as associate manager."

"I thought I was associate manager," said Chrissy.

"You're assistant manager."

"So Andrea would be over me?" Chrissy asked, her tone rising.

"Now let's not let our little egos get in the way of the good of the store," Richie said, his face suddenly becoming stern. "After all, the success of the store *is* our common goal."

"I thought Andrea had a job in a department store," Summyr said.

Richie frowned. "Yes, well, you know how the economy can be sometimes. It seems that her position was rather abruptly eliminated."

Probably the store didn't need her spritzing perfume on the customers as they walked in anymore, Summyr thought.

"That's no reflection on her abilities," Richie hurried to add. "After all, experts tell us that the average person will change careers three times in a lifetime."

"Perhaps even more often in Andrea's case," Summyr said, again trying to keep her tone neutral.

Richie stared for a moment, puzzled. "Ah, you mean that the more talented people will be in greater demand. Yes, I'm sure that's true."

"I don't like this, Richie." Chrissy's eyes had filed with tears, and she spoke in the solemn tone of a hurt little girl.

Richie went over and put his arm around her. "I know you don't, sweetheart, but this is for the good of the store. And just think how much you'll learn from being around Andrea. Do it for me, won't you?"

Chrissy nodded once without looking up.

"There is one problem, of course," Richie said, managing to make his face appear deeply saddened. "We can't afford to have three employees in addition to myself, so we'll have to let someone go. I'm afraid that means we won't be able to keep you on board, Summyr. I'm really sorry."

He walked towards her as if to give her a consoling hug, but Summyr put her hand in the center of his chest and stopped him.

"You can't do that, Richie," Chrissy said. "Summyr does lots of work around here. She's not afraid to get her hands dirty. I can't see Andrea being willing to lift boxes, not with that manicure."

"Now, now, let's not be catty," Richie said. "I'm sure that Andrea will be willing to do whatever work is included in her job description."

"I'm sure she will," Summyr said blandly. Going out with Richie was sure to be a large part of that description and probably the most unpleasant part.

"Fine. That's settled, then." Richie beamed at the

two women as if they were his best friends in the world.

Somewhere in that course he took they must have taught that if you keep smiling no one will hate you, Summyr thought.

Chrissy's expression was stony. "No, it's not set-tled. If Summyr goes, then . . ."

"It's all settled," Summyr interrupted.

"Good," Richie said quickly. "And you don't have to leave today, Summyr, you can stay until the end of the week. Andrea won't be starting until next Monday. We're going to Vermont for a little vacation until then."

Chrissy took a step backwards as if she'd been slapped.

"Andrea, darling, are you ready to go?" he called out.

Slowly, the woman walked down the aisle toward them, examining every inch of shelf as if she knew what she was looking at. Finally she finished her jour-ney to Richie's side.

"There's so much to do. I'm really excited at all the possibilities," she declared in a bored voice.

"Wonderful. Well, why don't we go get some lunch and let these folks get back to work," Richie said.

Andrea gave Richie a thin smile. Placing a posses-sive arm around her, he began walking up the aisle side-by-side with her. Almost immediately he knocked a bag of soy flour off a shelf, the aisles being far too narrow for such a romantic maneuver. Ignoring the bag, he dropped back a step and let Andrea go first as he followed along close behind.

"I don't know which one of them I feel sorry for the most." Then realizing that perhaps she wasn't being quite sensitive to her friend, Summyr turned to Chrissy, "Sorry, I guess I shouldn't have said that."

"Don't apologize. As much as I'd like to blame it all on that witch Andrea, Richie's as much to blame as she is. I guess I just thought that if I worked real hard and made myself indispensable around here that eventually he'd take an interest in me. I don't know why I thought it would work now, it's never worked before."

Summyr gave her friend a hug. The sign of friendship made Chrissy's eyes fill with tears.

"Don't worry," Summyr said. "You've got a lot to offer. Some day the right guy will come along and see that."

Chrissy gave a sniff. "Do you think it will be before I'm so old that I end up in a nursing home?" she said, attempting a smile.

"Don't be silly," Summyr said, returning her smile.

Sadly, she had to admit that Janet Benson had a point. Chrissy was in many ways a wonderful person. She was intelligent, hardworking, and had a dry sense of humor. But all of it came in a package that very few men would look at twice. The old saying that you shouldn't judge a book by its cover was true, but most people were more likely to read books with pretty covers. Also, if Chrissy had a bit more confidence in her appearance, maybe she wouldn't be so desperately inclined to chase losers like Richie.

"I'm sure you won't have to wait that long," Summyr said, trying to sound certain, but she was glad that Chrissy didn't look up to see the doubtful expression on her face.

"Why didn't you let me quit?" Chrissy asked. "It would serve Richie right for letting you go. And I don't want to work here all alone with Andrea."

"I didn't want you to quit until you've had some time to think about it. You were angry, and the decisions we make when we're angry aren't always the best. Besides, this way you can look around for another job before you leave."

"But what? I really enjoy what I'm doing here."

Summyr shrugged. "Then maybe you can outlast Andrea. Just do the same amount of work as you've always done. That will force Andrea to do my job in addition to whatever Richie thinks an associate manager should be doing. I'll bet that either Andrea gets tired of doing all that work and quits or refuses to do it. If Richie has to decide between keeping his do-nothing job or keeping Andrea, I think he'll pick laziness over love."

"Do you think so?" Chrissy said hopefully.

Summyr gave her a severe look. "No backsliding. Richie isn't worth chasing after. For Richie there will always be another Andrea. Even if you keep working here, find some other guy to get interested in."

"How?"

"You know how that works—some day, when you

least expect, he'll appear in your life from out of nowhere."

"Like Steve?" Chrissy's smile was teasing.

"Maybe," Summyr said. "It's too soon to tell. Anyway, right now I have other problems, like how I'm going to pay the bills and keep the yoga center without a job."

"Oh, that's right. I've been so busy feeling sorry for myself about Richie that I've been totally ignoring your problem. What are you going to do?"

"Look for another job, I guess."

"Isn't there some way that you could run the yoga center full time?"

Her uncle's offer to fund her in doing just that crossed Heather's mind, but once again she felt that she had to remain independent of her uncle if she didn't want to have problems with her father. He would never be happy if he knew that his daughter had to rely on his brother for financial support.

No, Summyr thought, there had to be another solution. But she had no idea at the moment what it might be.

Chapter Ten

The next morning Summyr was again surprised to find Steve waiting for her by the front door of the warehouse.

"Thought I'd get here early, before the crowd," he said with a grin.

"Yeah, there might actually be two or three in class this morning."

They walked into the warehouse. Summyr paused, trying to tell if something was wrong. She wondered if her senses were as sharp as they had been last night.

"What's the matter?" Steve asked.

She explained about finding the window open the previous night.

"Mind if I take a look?" he asked, switching on the warehouse-bay lights and heading toward the back.

"It was this one right here," Summyr said, when they came to the window in the far corner.

"And it was wide open? Not just unlocked."

"It was up about a foot. I think I must have felt the breeze somehow."

"All the way over by the front door?" he said doubtfully.

Summyr smiled. "I know, it seems pretty incredible. Maybe I was just unusually aware last night."

"I suppose it's possible. Who knows how the air currents move in a sealed-up place like this? A good thing you spotted it though, there aren't any neighbors on this side of the building. It would have been an open invitation to a break-in."

Steve stared out the window.

"Anything wrong?" she asked.

He shook his head and smiled. "Just thinking. I wonder who left it open?"

"Probably Schuster."

"Has he been around again?"

Summyr told him about the man's fall from the ladder.

Steve shook his head. "This certainly has been a busy place. And he just fell off the ladder by accident?"

"That's what he said."

"Not a good thing in a contractor," Steve said, smiling. "You'd at least expect him to be able to stay on a ladder."

"Well, he isn't exactly the most agile guy around, and he's way too heavy for my aluminum five-footer."

"And that happened yesterday morning, but you found the window open last night."

Summyr nodded. "Of course, the window could have been open all day. I might have missed it in the morning when they were carrying Schuster out. With the front door open I wouldn't have felt the breeze from back here."

"So Schuster could have opened the window, forgotten about it, and then gone upstairs where he fell from the ladder," Steve said.

Summyr detected a note of doubt in his voice. "You don't think that's the way it happened?"

"Of course, it could have happened that way," Steve said, leading the way back to the front of the warehouse. "I just don't see why Schuster would have opened the window if he was going to head upstairs."

"The man didn't seem very organized. After all, he didn't even have his own ladder."

Steve laughed. "You're right. It's probably pointless to try to figure out why a man like that does anything."

They climbed up the stairs and Summyr opened the door to the yoga center. She went over to her desk and began listening to her phone messages, while Steve took off his shoes. There were two messages from prospective new students. Summyr wondered whether it was even worthwhile to take on new people, given the precarious future of the business.

"You look sad," Steve said.

He was staring at her with such a concerned expression that Summyr smiled.

"I lost my job today," she said, and told him about the scene at Root and Branch.

"Sounds like you're better off not working for that jerk, but I realize that the job was important to you. Perhaps something better will come along."

"I hope so. I'll probably have to pay more rent wherever I relocate from here."

"And that's in just three weeks."

"Don't remind me."

Steve stood up and walked over to stand right in front of the desk.

"Why don't you let me take your mind off your troubles, for a little while at least. I've been intending to ask you out again. I would have talked to you after the last class, but I've been so busy lately that I didn't know when I'd be free."

He shifted slightly toward his right and the light from the window caught him full in the face. Summyr saw dark circles under his eyes and new lines etched into his forehead.

"You look exhausted."

"Yeah. I've been putting in a lot of extra hours this week. I'm covering for someone who's sick."

"Has your shoulder been bothering you?"

He nodded. A look of annoyance flashed across his usually placid face, showing that he didn't like to talk about how much the disability was costing him.

"When I have to remain in the same position for a long time, it stiffens up and starts to get to me," he admitted.

"That's going to happen for a while. You have to be patient with your body."

"I guess patience has never been my greatest strength."

"I'd have thought you could be very patient when you had to be," said Summyr.

"That's true. If I want something enough, I can be very patient and very persistent. For example, if you refused to go out with me for dinner tonight, which I'll admit is very short notice, I would keep asking and asking."

"Well, you won't have your patience tested this time," said Summyr. "Because it just so happens that you're in luck. Normally I would be working at the store on Friday night, but since Saturday is my last day, I decided to take Friday night off and do something special."

"Ah, so you've already made other plans."

"In a sense. I was planning to make myself a really nice meal at home."

"Vegetarian, I'll bet."

"Probably. Will that stop you from coming over to my place for dinner tonight?"

Steve reached out and took her hand. "Summyr, if you were frying up tree bark and having it with a side order of poison ivy leaves stuffed with crab grass, I'd still be pleased to dine with you."

Summyr suppressed a smile. "I might be able to do a bit better than that, and unfortunately, poison ivy isn't in season."

"Then maybe we can do this again when it is," Steve said solemnly.

Summyr wrote down her address and handed it across the desk. The setting seemed oddly formal for arranging a date.

"Around seven."

"I'll be there. Is there anything you'd like me to bring?"

"Just your appetite."

Their eyes met and slowly they both leaned forward across the desk. Good thing we're both tall or we could lose our balance, Summyr thought, as their lips gently touched. They pulled away quickly at the sound of footsteps coming up the stairs. Summyr had expected to see Janet Benson appear in the doorway, bursting with chatter as usual, but instead it was Alicia Molloy. The woman said hello to Summyr. Steve seemed suddenly involved with looking out the window, but once Alicia turned to go into the studio his eyes followed her carefully.

"Still fascinated by her?" Summyr asked in a whisper. She couldn't believe she'd said that, but suddenly Steve's obvious interest in Alicia was intolerable.

"Sorry," he whispered back. "But it isn't what it looks like."

"What does that mean?"

"I can't tell you right now."

"You'd better be able to tell me tonight," she replied, walking past him and into the yoga studio.

The class was very small. Janet Benson never did appear. Fortunately one older woman with a cane, and a student from the college arrived just as the class was about to begin. Summyr breathed a silent sigh of relief. Having a class with just Steve, Alicia, and herself somehow seemed just a bit too strange. The "triangle" posture in yoga wasn't meant to be a love triangle.

By carefully focusing on her breath and putting more concentration than usual into the postures, Summyr was able to relax. Gradually all of her recent anxieties seemed to float away, and she could even look at the beautiful and shapely Alicia with only a tiny twinge of envy and suspicion. When the rest of the class went into 'threading the needle' posture, she slipped over to Steve's side.

"Why don't you do a spinal twist instead? "Threading the needle" will be too much for your shoulder."

"I really can explain," he whispered.

"Later," she replied sternly and returned to her rug in the front of the room.

When the class was done, she half-expected that Steve would stay behind to give his promised explanation. Instead he quickly said, "See you tonight," and left right behind Alicia.

What *is* going on here, Summyr wondered. He doesn't seem like the kind of guy who chases every woman he lays eyes on, but he seems obsessed with Alicia. But the first time he saw Alicia he had speculated on her vanity. Was he the kind of man who found vain women to be some kind of a romantic challenge? But then why is he coming to dinner with me? I may be a lot of things, but vain isn't one of them.

Questions without answers swirled through Summyr's head until she finally decided that she should practice a little patience herself. Tonight she would have answers or else not see Steve again. He might be fun, but she wasn't going to get involved with someone she couldn't trust. Some women liked the kind of man where you never knew where you stood, but that had never been Summyr's ideal.

She locked up the yoga studio. On her way out of the warehouse, she took the time to make a careful survey of the windows. All of them were closed and locked. Although the warped metal window frames didn't give much confidence that they would stand up to a determined prowler, Summyr figured that she only had to worry about it for three weeks and they should do the trick until then.

Pulling out of the parking lot, she turned to go into town to pick up some of the ingredients for the dinner at the new supermarket that recently had opened right off the center green. Summyr had decided on pasta with ricotta and walnut sauce with a big green salad to accompany it. The meal would be filling and tasty.

But what about dessert? She toyed for a moment with the idea of whipping up some tofu rice pudding, but figured that would be asking a lot of any nonvegetarian. When she got to the supermarket, she purchased the parmesan and ricotta cheese, the walnuts, and the salad fixings, then decided that a good quality chocolate ice cream might be just the reward for someone who still had their training wheels on when it came to a vegetarian menu.

As Summyr was walking across the parking lot, a

car stopped beside her. The widow rolled down to reveal her uncle's smiling face.

"How are you today, niece?" he asked with a slightly silly grin. "A beautiful day in the neighborhood, isn't it."

A chilly breeze was blowing across the parking lot for April, but Summyr nodded, deciding that it was certainly a lovely day in her uncle's heart.

"How was your date last night?" she asked.

The smile grew even wider. "Wonderful. We had a great time. After dinner we talked and talked. It's been years since I talked to anyone like that." He paused for a moment. "Maybe, never."

Summyr nodded. Her mother had told her that after she started going out with Summyr's father and even after they married, Harold still used to call her to discuss his plans for the future. She had always treated him like a much-loved brother, but wished that he could find a women of his own to confide in.

"It must be hard to get used to talking to another person that way."

"Not with Babe. With her it's easy."

"Babe?"

Uncle Harold gave a sheepish smile. "That's her nickname."

"I see," Summyr said, picturing in her mind an over-the-hill Las Vegas showgirl with somewhat tarnished sequins.

"Looks like you've been doing some shopping," Uncle Harold said.

"Yes. As a matter of fact I have a date tonight myself."

"Good." Her uncle's face turned serious. "It's about time you starting dating again. Looks like we're both getting back on track at the same time. Of course, it took me a lot longer."

A car pulled up behind her uncle and gave an impatient beep. Her uncle slowly pulled away.

"I'd like you to meet Babe," he called. "We'll have to get together soon. Oh, by the way, I checked on Louie Schuster for you. He did break his leg, but there's no indication that he plans to sue."

As he drove away, Summyr realized that she hadn't told him about losing her job. She would have to inform him soon because it could have a serious impact on her ability to rent a new studio. But there was no point in raining on his parade now. He'd waited a long time to find someone, and he certainly deserved a few days of undisturbed happiness. She only hoped that he had found the right person.

Although she wasn't working that evening, Summyr had promised Chrissy that she would work the afternoon, because several large shipments were expected to arrive. When she got to Root and Branch, Chrissy was pacing back and forth behind the counter.

"What's the matter?" Summyr asked as she hung up her coat.

"Janet Benson was just in here. When I told her about Richie hiring Andrea, she got all upset. She said that I was letting him treat me like dirt and that I should find another place to work."

"What did you say?"

"I said that all sounded fine, but I liked working in a health-food store. This kind of stuff really interests me, and it wouldn't be easy to find another position. The only other one in town doesn't need anyone."

"How do you know that?"

Chrissy looked guilty. "I called over and spoke to Maggie yesterday. She'd like to hire me, but she's already got all the staff she needs."

"So you are planning to leave?"

"Sort of. After we talked yesterday I got to thinking that you were probably right, even if I outlasted Andrea, it would only be a matter of time and then there would be another Andrea. Richie doesn't care about me as a person. He only acts nice to me because I do most of his work for him. If I'm going to work that hard, I want more to show for it. If I can't have Richie, at least I can have a decent career."

"What did Janet say when you told her that another job wouldn't be easy to find?" asked Summyr.

"That's when it got really strange. She asked me how I would like to go into a partnership with her."

"What sort of a partnership?"

"Running a store just like this one. Janet said that she would supply the space and the start-up money, and she'd hire me to run it. I'd own a quarter of the business, and she'd own the rest. I'd get a small salary as manager and a quarter of the profits."

Summyr gave her friend a congratulatory hug. "Sounds like a good deal. Why all the pacing? Running your own store is exactly what you've always wanted to do, isn't it?"

"Yeah, I guess. But it's all kind of sudden. I'm not even sure that I can do it. And Janet said that if I was going to be a manager, I had to look more professional. She made an appointment for me at Loretta's for today at five."

"Loretta's. Isn't that the stylish beauty salon?"

Chrissy nodded anxiously. "Can you take over for me until closing?"

Closing was six o'clock. Summyr rapidly calculated how long it would take to prepare dinner.

"Sure, I can do that. Have a good time. You'll enjoy getting yourself all fixed up."

"I'm not so sure." Chrissy leaned closer and dropped her voice. "You know I've never been to a beauty parlor."

"Never?"

She shook her head. "Mom always said that was for women who were stuck on themselves. Dad always cut her hair, and she cut mine."

Summyr glanced at Chrissy's tangled mass of hair and kept silent.

"Well, I think you'll find that lots of women who are pretty normal get their hair done at a beauty salon," Summyr said. "It's not a matter of being proud, more a question of just feeling good because you look good."

"You think so?"

"Sure. And remember, you're not doing it because

you're conceited, you're doing it because you have to as part of the job."

"That's true," Chrissy said.

"You might find that cosmetics might even help give you a more professional look, and maybe a couple of new outfits," Summyr suggested. "After all, as a manager of your own store you'll have to set the right tone."

"Manager of my own store," Chrissy said wistfully. "That sounds really nice, but a little scary at the same time."

"Don't worry. You'll do fine. It won't be any harder than what you've been doing here for years, and now you'll be working for yourself."

The doorbell in the back rang, indicating that a truck had arrived with a delivery.

"There's one thing I'm not going to do, though, even if I take Janet up on her offer," Chrissy said, as they hurried toward the rear of the store.

"What's that?"

"Get those phony nails like Andrea."

"Why not?"

"Because even if I'm a manager and part-owner, I still want to be able to do the work."

Chapter Eleven

Summyr had just completed putting the finishing touches on the salad when the bell rang. When she opened the door, Steve held a large bouquet of spring flowers out in front of him.

"This is for decoration, not for eating," he said with a mischievous smile.

"Some flowers are very edible," Summyr replied, as he stepped into the apartment.

"I hope you weren't planning to serve flowers for dinner, or I've already gotten off on the wrong foot."

"Not this time. But now that I know that you like to munch on a good nasturtium, I'll see what I can do."

Steve grinned. Summyr realized once again how handsome he was with his black wavy hair, slim waist and broad shoulders, and open smile, all of it made more poignant by the scar that ran down his cheek. He was wearing a gray turtleneck with a blue blazer, which gave him kind of a nautical look. A pirate who was trying to fit in around the yacht basin, Summyr thought, smiling to herself.

"What's so funny?" Steve asked.

"Nothing."

"You can't fool me, I saw your lips twitch."

"I was just thinking how dashing you look."

Steve gave her a suspicious look. "I think I'm getting the censored version of your thoughts, because I'm not sure why dashing would make you smile. Do I look ridiculous in some way?"

"You just look different."

"Ah, that might be because you usually see me in yoga class where I'm wearing just a T-shirt and gym shorts. Next time I'll wear a tux to class. A man should always try to appear dashing."

"You look just fine in the T-shirt and gym shorts," said Summyr.

His eyes sparkled with mischief. "I didn't think you noticed. Isn't that a violation of the yoga teacher code or something?"

"A good yoga teacher notices everything, but only comments on those things that matter," said Summyr, folding her hands in front of her chest in prayer position and looking solemn.

Steve laughed. "Now I'll always be worried in class because I'll figure that I'm making lots of mistakes, but you think that I'm too hopeless to be worth correcting."

"Don't worry. I'll give you lots of corrections."

They walked into the center of the living room, part of which also served as a dining room. Summyr's third floor apartment consisted of one rather large room devoted to the living and dining area. Down a short hall was a bedroom and bath. A small but efficient galley kitchen ran off the dining area.

"Nice room," Steve said. "Very warm and cozy." He walked over to an end table and picked up a picture of a couple. "Your parents?"

Summyr nodded. "My father is in Florida. My mother died five years ago."

"I'm sorry," said Steve.

"Yes. She was a very warm and funny woman."

"You must take after her."

"When I'm at my best. My father is very funny as well, but he's much more gregarious. He was a musician, and he likes to be surrounded by people. He works at a retirement community as the recreation director."

"That must be a tough job."

Summyr nodded. "But it's perfect for him. The tougher the audience, the more he likes it."

"So you're the daughter of a musician. I can see why you're looking for a stable guy."

Summyr ignored his comment and walked over to the French doors at one end of the room.

"The apartment isn't anything special, except for this." Summyr threw open the French doors to reveal a small balcony.

They walked out on the balcony. Steve leaned on the wrought-iron railing and looked into the distance.

"You can make out the tallest trees on the green. The steeple on the Congregational Church is to your right, and on a clear day you can even see the skyscrapers in Springfield," Summyr said.

They stood next to each other in companionable silence and took in the view. It was one of those early spring evenings when you can smell the moist earth getting ready to bring forth another season of growth. A cool breeze ruffled the curtains on the doors, and Summyr shivered slightly. Steve put an arm around her.

"Cold?"

"Not really. The breeze just caught me by surprise." She leaned into his arm and suddenly felt very relaxed.

"You have a wonderful spot here," Steve said. After a moment he continued, "Why did you frown a moment ago when I said that you were looking for a stable guy? Isn't that what you told me?"

"I did. It's just that I've been doing a lot of thinking since."

"And now you're looking for someone who's wild and crazy?"

Summyr grinned. "I've been thinking, not losing my senses. It's just that people have been saying that John was really a very funny guy and that was what attracted me to him."

"What's wrong with that?"

"Nothing, really. It's just that after he died somehow I kept thinking that he had provided stability in my life, and that's why I fell in love with him. I guess I kind of forgot about everything else."

"There's nothing odd about that. Your mother dies, your father moves to Florida, and then your fiancé is killed: I can see why you might think that you'd lost the last person you could count on."

"I can always count on myself," Summyr said quickly.

"And that's important. But life is a lot easier if you have someone else to help you."

Summyr turned to face him and suddenly they were looking directly into each other's eyes. Steve reached forward and, taking her by the shoulders, he drew her towards him. When their faces were only inches away, before he could bend his head toward hers, Summyr moved forward and raised her face, pressing her lips against his. Steve made a small sound of surprise, then his arms pulled her into him and she relaxed into the firmness of his body. Her senses drifted as she focused solely on the warmth of the kiss.

When they disentangled, Summyr smiled. "Well, that was certainly . . . nice."

"Nice?" Steve said with a pretended look of injury. "I was expecting 'spectacular' or 'marvelous'. I was even hoping for 'unsurpassed.' "

"Hmm. You expect a lot for a first kiss."

"Maybe I just need a bit more practice," he suggested, moving toward her again.

She put up a hand to stop him. "Not until after dinner."

"Oh, yes. Nothing like devouring a few plants to build up a man's ardor."

"Stop complaining until you've tried it," said Summyr. "And if you eat everything on your plate, you'll get some dessert."

"And what will that be? Something carved out of tofu?"

Summyr laughed, but thanked her lucky stars that she had rejected the idea of the tofu rice pudding.

"You know, that was really excellent," Steve said a little over an hour later, as he finished the last of his ice cream. "The pasta was superb. I never would have thought of having it any other way than with tomato sauce, but this was really something special. And who thinks of pasta as a vegetarian dish?"

Summyr nodded. "Everyone thinks food has to be something weird if it's vegetarian. Of course, there are some unusual dishes, but many of them are quite normal with a substitution of some other source of protein for the meat. In this case, the nuts and cheese."

Steve patted his stomach. "And as a guy gets older, he has to watch his diet more and more."

"You're hardly overweight."

"Yeah. But I've put on a couple of pounds since I hurt my arm. I can't do all the things in the gym that I'd like to do."

"You're working out in the gym as well as practicing yoga?"

Steve gave a slightly sheepish smile. "I guess I've got kind of a thing about staying in shape."

"So you can lift those heavy sample cases," Summyr teased.

"Right," he said quickly.

But Summyr noticed that he didn't smile, and she was afraid she'd hurt his feelings.

"Does the arm bother you on the job?"

"Sometimes. It has been getting better, but I'm not sure that it will ever be back to normal."

"Could you find another job? One where you didn't have to use the shoulder as much?"

"I suppose. But I really like what I do."

He said this with such quiet intensity that Summyr decided to change the subject, and they discussed Chrissy's opportunity to run her own store.

"Too bad you can't give your full attention to the yoga studio. That's really what you're passionate about doing, isn't it?" Steve said.

"Maybe someday that will happen. Right now, I'm more concerned about finding a new space to rent."

Summyr got up and began to clear the table. Steve immediately jumped to his feet to give her a hand.

"How did you ever end up in the old Consolidated Trucking warehouse, anyway?" he asked as they stood side by side at the kitchen counter.

"Is that what was in there before? How did you know?"

Steve shrugged. "Guess I just remember what used to be there."

"Didn't they have some kind of problem with the police?" Summyr asked. "I seem to recall something in the papers about three years ago. I think the company bookkeeper embezzled funds or something like that. They never found out what happened to the money and the company went out of business."

"Sounds right," Steve said, carefully cleaning off the plates into the garbage bin.

"I never knew that was the same building."

"Well, they were gone long before you rented there."

Steve insisted that he be allowed to wash the dishes, while Summyr dried and put them away. He said that he didn't want to be one of those guests you didn't invite back because it took hours to clean up after he left. When they were done, they returned to the living room and sat next to each other on the sofa. Steve's arm came around her shoulders, and Summyr kicked off her shoes and curled her feet under her, leaning into him.

"Time for more practice," Steve said, waggling his eyebrows lecherously.

"Before that, you still have to answer one more question for me."

"And that would be?"

"What about Alicia? You said you were going to explain why you seem so fascinated by her."

"Jealous, are we?"

"Let's just say that I don't go out with guys who are looking at another woman at the same time they're talking to me."

"Okay," Steve said. "You see a friend of mine, Jim, is interested in Alicia. So I've been keeping an eye on her."

"This friend has you spying on her?" Summyr asked, twisting around so she could see Steve's face.

"No. It's nothing like that. I told him that I was in the yoga class, and he asked if I'd met his girlfriend. I told him that I'd seen her."

Summyr gave him a skeptical look.

"Well, let me put it this way, if you were in a class with a boyfriend of some girl you were friendly with, wouldn't you pay particular attention to him? Kind of try to decide if he was good enough for your friend?"

"I might. But I didn't know guys thought that way."

"Some of us do," Steve said.

"And that's all there is to it?"

Steve nodded.

"I guess I know what you mean. I'd really like to meet this woman who's going out with my uncle."

"So you see, I'm not being so unreasonable after all. Nobody wants a friend or relative to get hurt in a bad relationship."

"I'm especially worried that she might be lying to him," Summyr said.

"Why would she do that?"

"Uncle Harold isn't a very experienced person when it comes to women. Maybe this Babe woman saw that and figured she could take advantage of his naiveté."

"I suppose it's possible."

"There's nothing I like less than a liar," Summyr said, suddenly outraged at the thought of this unscrupulous woman who was trying to deceive her uncle. "I think that if a person lies to someone that's about the worst thing you can do."

Steve was silent.

"Don't you agree with me?"

"I agree that lying is usually wrong. But I'm not sure that it's the *worst* thing you can do to someone. And I think that maybe you're jumping to conclusions about your uncle's girlfriend. Shouldn't you wait to meet her before you decide that she's a conniving witch?"

Summyr smiled sheepishly. "I guess you're right. I just get awfully protective when it comes to my uncle. He's a really sweet, gentle guy who happens to have a silly romantic streak a mile wide. And he's been good to me over the years. I'd hate to see him hurt."

"That just proves what a nice person you are. But maybe it's time we stopped talking for a while," Steve said, moving his face closer to hers.

Any further worries Summyr had soon became lost in the feelings of the moment.

Chapter Twelve

The next morning the sun was shining through her bedroom window when Summyr awoke. She felt happy as she stretched languorously, still half-asleep. She savored the feeling for a moment, not even considering the source. Then the memory of her evening with Steve came rushing back, sweeping through her mind like a hot breeze. By the time he left it had been close to midnight. They had talked and kissed for hours, torn between wanting to learn more about each other and at the same time wanting to be physically close.

She closed her eyes and pictured his face: the handsome features marred only by the scar on his cheek. But perhaps "marred" was the wrong word. Somehow the fact that he managed to handle his disfigurement with equanimity and even humor made him more attractive to her. Yoga had taught Summyr that physical beauty is fleeting; it's the beauty within that is most important. This was what she saw in Steve.

Summyr closed her eyes again, pressing them tight, and this time managed to conjure up an image of John. His picture was still on the top of her night table, but she wanted to test her memory. Slowly he came into focus. She knew that her love for him would outlast her fading ability to picture his face, but right now it seemed important to Summyr to compare his image with that of Steve.

They couldn't have appeared more different. Whereas Steve was tall with dark hair and a wide smile, John had been shorter and blond, and he had grinned more frequently than he smiled. Even when John thought something was very funny, it would be shown more by a crooked grin than outright laughter. His blue eyes would dance with humor, but rarely did it come out in a loud display. He enjoyed making others laugh more than laughing himself.

Two very different men, Summyr concluded. Steve was open with his emotions and quick to urge her to show her feelings as well. John had been more reticent and more serious, a bit more like Summyr herself. Perhaps their similarity would have been a problem once they were married; two earnest people could make for a rather somber marriage. But there was still something about Steve that gave her second thoughts. Despite all their talk last night, she still didn't feel that she really knew him. When he talked about his life, Summyr felt that she was seeing a partially completed painting of a still life where the background was completely filled in but the central figure remained sketchy and obscure. She had learned a lot of rather trivial facts about who he was, but the central mystery seemed to remain.

Sighing, Summyr climbed out of bed. Saturday was not a day of rest. There was a yoga class to teach this morning, and she was going to be putting in her last day at Root and Branch. After showering and having breakfast, Summyr drove to the yoga studio. In the parking lot she stood by her car for a moment and looked around the neighborhood. An area with a mix of small factories and some office buildings, it was unusually quiet on a weekend, and Summyr paused to enjoy the peace. After watching a spring robin hop across the driveway, heading for the scrap of battered lawn next to her building, Summyr decided that it was time for her to get to work as well.

She had just finished listening to the messages on her answering machine and giving the carpet a quick vacuum when the first students began to arrive. Saturday's class was usually big, and today was no exception. Over fifteen students were there by the time class began, brought out, no doubt, by a combination of the convenient time and a beautiful spring morning. Even Alicia seemed happier than usual, and gave Summyr a friendly nod as she came in. She knew Steve wouldn't be there because he had said that all his recent overtime made Saturday a time for getting his unfinished errands done. By the time class was over at eleven-thirty, Summyr was tired. Many of the

students had been newcomers requiring
tion of the postures and very close sup

As the last of the newcomers, a blond
in her early twenties, was about to leav
Summyr, "Didn't I see you at the General Knox Inn
the other day? You were with Steve Rafferty, right?"

Summyr nodded cautiously. Could this be one of
Steve's former girlfriends? She looked a bit young, but
a guy as handsome as Steve would probably appeal to
a pretty wide age-group.

"Steve's a great guy, isn't he? I was going to come
over and speak to him, but I work in the kitchen and
I couldn't get free," said the young woman.

"How do you know him?" Summyr asked, smiling
politely and bracing herself for the worst.

"I graduated from college two years ago. I was a
criminal justice major and did my internship in the
Springfield Police Department. Steve was my super-
visor."

"Steve's a cop?" Summyr blurted out.

"Sure," the woman answered, puzzled. "You didn't
know that?"

For a moment Summyr could see herself through
the other woman's eyes. Here she was having lunch
with a guy, and she didn't even know his occupation.
Of course, it wasn't that I hadn't asked, Summyr
thought. He had stood right here in the yoga studio
and told me that he sold pharmaceuticals. Why would
anyone expect him to lie about that? You might lie
about being a movie star, but a drug salesman?

"I guess it never came up," Summyr said lamely. "Steve takes a class here, and that's how I know him."

The woman smiled and nodded, obviously still not convinced that Summyr wasn't a bit slow.

"Well, tell him Debbie Merino says hello when you talk to him again," she said.

"I'll do that."

When Summyr was alone, she sank down in the chair behind her desk and stared out the window, unseeing. How could Steve have lied to her like that? It hadn't been a simple lie either. He had made up a completely different profession for himself and fabricated the details of his daily routine. Why would he do that? Was he some kind of pathological liar who enjoyed going through life inventing new identities?

Summyr took a deep breath and tried to center herself. She was clearly letting her thoughts run away with her. If Steve was a cop, he was probably not pathological. That meant he must have had a more conventional reason to lie, but what could it be? She cast her mind back to their first conversation when he was about to fill out his class registration form. They had just been talking about . . . about John, and how he had died. Is it possible, Summyr wondered, that Steve didn't think she'd go out with him if he admitted to having a dangerous profession, so he'd lied and said that he was a salesman? Then maybe he lied about how he injured his shoulder as well? Could the injury be the result of a bullet or knife wound rather than an auto accident?

Summyr closed her eyes and took some more calming breaths. He lied, so he's a liar. The statement raced through her mind with crushing logic. Even though she had told him that she demanded honesty in a man, he had told her lies. And then just last night, when she had expressed her concerns about Uncle Harold's girlfriend possibly being deceitful, he had sympathized, all the while knowing that he had told her the most outrageous story. No wonder I felt that I didn't really know him, she thought, it was all an act.

Summyr pulled open her top file drawer. Her fingers trembled with anger as she leafed through the last month's registration forms until she came to Steve's. Her fingers punched in the keys of his number as if she wished her finger were poking into his chest.

"Hello," a woman's voice answered.

Was she about to find out that he had a wife, too? The ultimate lie.

"May I speak to Steve, please?" Summyr said. She tried to keep her voice from quivering, but she was certain that it sounded full of emotion.

"I'm sorry, but Steve hasn't lived here for a number of years."

"Oh?"

"This is his mother. Steve has an apartment in Springfield. You must not have talked to Steve in a long time."

Not the real one, anyway.

"Could you give me his number in Springfield?" Summyr asked.

"And you are?"

"Summyr Fox. Steve is taking a yoga class at my

studio, and I wanted to let him know about a change in the class schedule." How easy it is to lie, Summyr thought, shocked at how easily the improvised story had come from her lips.

There was a short pause. "Well, I can't see any harm in that," the woman said, and rattled off a phone number.

After she had thanked Steve's mother and hung up, Summyr sat for a moment with her finger poised over the telephone. Her initial inclination had been to call Steve, let him know exactly what her candid opinion was of guys who lied to her, and say she never wanted to see him again. But what if Steve had lied because he thought she wouldn't go out with him otherwise? That was still wrong, but didn't it show that he cared? By the time she punched in the number, Summyr was not ready to forgive and forget, but she was willing to listen.

She twisted the phone cord nervously as it rang on the other end. After four rings, Steve's voice came on, repeated the number, and asked for the caller to leave a message. She considered just hanging up and waiting until she caught him at home. But a sudden surge of anger came over her.

"Steve, this is Summyr. Perhaps you'd give me a call when you have a chance and try to explain why you lied to me about being on the police force."

After she hung up, she felt a bit guilty about the abruptness of her message. Then she reminded herself that he had systematically lied to her, and there was no reason to go easy on him until she had proof that his behavior wasn't as bad as it seemed. She looked at her watch. It was time to go off to Root and Branch. Maybe I can talk over this whole thing with Chrissy, Summyr thought. Of course, she'll probably tell me to forgive Steve for everything because he's cute.

When Summyr pulled into the parking lot of Root and Branch, she was surprised to see Richie's car in its usual spot near the front door. Wasn't he supposed to be spending the weekend in Vermont with Andrea?

"I'm just not interested. That's what I said. What part of that didn't you understand?"

The words echoed around the small shop. Summyr paused by the front counter, which was unstaffed. The voice had definitely been Chrissy's, but the tone had been firmer and more aggressive than Summyr had ever heard before.

"C'mon, Chrissy, don't be silly. I'm willing to let things go back to the way they were," Richie said.

"Maybe the way they were isn't going to cut it any-more, Richie."

"Okay, okay, I can understand how your feelings might be a little hurt. I'm willing to make it up to you. What if I make you associate manager?"

"Titles are meaningless unless more money comes along with it," Chrissy said.

"My hands are tied. We've got to show a profit."

"I'll bet your hands weren't tied when it came to Andrea." Chrissy paused to let the double entendre sink in. "How much were you going to offer her?"

"That was different."

"Because she was cute and you were going out with her."

There was a long moment of silence. Probably Richie trying to remember the "how to handle employee dissatisfaction" section from his one college course, Summyr guessed.

"Fair enough," he finally replied, in a tone more tired than calm. "Let's say I give you an extra twenty-five dollars a week."

"Fifty."

"Be reasonable, Chrissy."

"Associate manager and fifty dollars a week, then I'll think about it."

"All right," he said so softly that Summyr could barely hear him.

"Good," Chrissy said with a note of triumph in her voice. "Well, I've thought about it, and I'm still not interested."

"What!" Richie yelped. "You're going to pass up a great opportunity like this?"

"Let me understand this great opportunity," Chrissy said slowly, the sarcasm obvious. "Your girlfriend of five days has dumped you and gotten a job at another department store. So I'm supposed to ignore the fact that you were going to bring her in from the outside and promote her over me, the one who has done most of the work around here for the last three years while you've done nothing but loaf around. Now that you're finally willing to give me the title and the salary increase that I should have had two years ago, you expect me to be thankful. Is that right?"

"Hey, that's not fair. We've always been partners. The store has always been more important than any individual's selfish interest."

"It's never been more important than yours," Chrissy shot back. "I've been a fool, and I admit it. I should have left here years ago, but I got too comfortable. Too comfortable with the job, and too comfortable with all your cheap flattery."

"Well, if that's the way you feel, maybe you should find yourself another job," Richie said.

"Okay, then, I will."

"You won't find it so easy out there, Chrissy. You aren't exactly going to get by on your looks." There was a long pause. Summyr wondered whether Richie was feeling sorry for what he said. "Although you do look more together today somehow," he admitted in a slightly surprised tone.

"Thanks," Chrissy said. "So let's figure that I've given you my two weeks notice. You'd better start looking for my replacement, so I can train her before I leave."

"C'mon, Chrissy, won't you just give me one more chance?"

"You're using that line on the wrong person. You should be talking to Andrea."

"Okay, okay, go then," Richie snapped. "In fact, why don't you leave right now. That way I won't have to see you again. But don't come back here crying, asking for your old job back. Once you walk out that door, it's all over between us."

Chrissy gave a sharp laugh. "Richie, there was never anything between us."

Chrissy walked down the aisle toward the counter. Summyr hardly recognized her. Her hair had been cut so that it swung bouncily at chin length. Her face had been made up to give her some color and a professional appearance. Even her shirttail was neatly tucked in to a pair of slacks that seemed to fit. Although her lips were trembling a little as she marched toward the counter, she managed to give Summyr a surreptitious wink as she slipped the coiled elastic that held the cash register key off of her wrist and placed it in the center of the counter.

Richie came down the aisle behind her. He looked concerned, as if he had just encountered something that neither his college course or his natural charm had prepared him to handle.

"I'll expect to receive my check for this week in the mail," Chrissy said.

Richie's face brightened. "Well, Summyr, I guess every cloud has a silver lining. This means you get to keep your job. In fact I'll promote you to assistant manager, Chrissy's old position."

"Not even associate?" Summyr asked.

Richie lips went thin and he turned red. "All right, all right. Everyone is taking advantage of my good nature today. You're associate manager."

"Sorry, Richie, but you've already fired me. Today is my last day."

"I'm unfiring you."

Summyr shook her head. "I've made other plans."

"Wait a minute. You're leaving and Chrissy is leaving. Who's going to run the store?" he asked.

"You'd better be here at nine o'clock on Monday morning or the store won't open," Chrissy said gently, almost as if she felt sorry for him

He stared at the two women, the reality of the situation slowly dawning on him. He turned and stalked out of the store. His car left the parking lot a few seconds later with tires squealing.

"Poor jerk," Chrissy said. "This is one problem he can't run away from."

"Maybe he'll manage to con another woman into taking over the shop."

Chrissy shrugged. "That's not my problem anymore."

"So you're going to go into business with Janet?"

"Yes. I told her when we went together to have my hair done yesterday. By the way, how do you like it?"

"Looks great."

"Yeah, I think so, too. We bought some makeup, and she showed me how to use it. We stopped at that little clothing store downtown, and I got this pair of slacks and a skirt. Then we had dinner and a long talk. Unlike Richie's extra fifty dollars and a smile, I think that Janet's offer really is a great opportunity."

Summyr reached out and put her hand on her friend's shoulder. "Well, then, congratulations and good luck."

"Thanks. By the way, you could have taken Richie up on his offer. I wouldn't have been offended if you took over my old job. You'd probably do a better job than I ever did of getting Richie to treat you right."

"It wouldn't be the same around here without you. I'd have to work too hard," Summyr said with a smile. Then her face turned serious. "And I guess I feel that maybe my life has come to a turning point as well. Ever since John died, I've been kind of going along on autopilot. Just getting up and doing whatever needed to be done, not thinking about whether I should try something new. But now I think that I'm ready. I'm not sure what for, but I feel that I'm ready for something new."

Chrissy nodded. "Look, I'd better get out of here; I've just been fired. I'll give you a call, and we can get together in the next couple of days."

Chrissy looked up and down the store one final time, then slipped into her coat. Giving Summyr a hug, she left.

It was only when the door had closed behind her that Summyr remembered that she hadn't told her about Steve being a cop. Although she hadn't put much stock in Chrissy's advice on the way over, what she had seen in the last few minutes made her think that perhaps Chrissy would prove a better source of advice in the future.

Chapter Thirteen

When five o'clock rolled around, Summyr locked up the store. She had placed Chrissy's key in the security box under the cash register. She'd return her own key sometime next week. As Summyr drove home, she wondered what she should do with the rest of the night: a Saturday night with nothing to do. It certainly wouldn't be the first, but meeting Steve had made her dissatisfied with the monotonous course her social life had taken over the last year or so. Now that she had been jolted out of her complacent rut there would be no going back again.

When she got home there was a message on her answering machine. Hoping that it was Steve, she excitedly pushed the button.

"Hi Summyr, it's Dad. Can you give me a call back as soon as you get a chance?"

All sorts of medical emergencies flashed through Summyr's mind as she punched in her father's number.

"Hi, Dad, what's wrong?" she asked breathlessly when he picked up the phone.

"Nothing's wrong, sweetheart, how are you?"

She took a deep breath, but didn't really relax. Her father could be about to go on life support, and he'd deny having a problem. Dad's motto had always been "never let them see you sweat."

"I'm fine. Now why don't you tell me why you called?" she said firmly.

Her father chuckled. "Glad to see you haven't changed. You still cut right to the chase."

"And this time the chase would be?" she asked.

"I'm getting married."

Summyr paused. She looked through the French doors and out across to the town center. There was a haze of green surrounding the trees. Was it the buds getting ready to burst into bloom or her own vision getting fuzzy from the shock of her father's news?

"Are you still there, Summyr?" he asked.

"Congratulations," she stammered. "Who's the lucky woman?"

"Her name is Gina. She works here at the community. She used to be a singer."

"A singer," said Summyr. "I guess you always had a weakness for them."

Her father gave a low laugh. "No one will ever replace your mother, Summyr, you know that. She'll always have star billing in my heart. But I'm no good at living alone. And Gina's real nice. We met when we decided to entertain the old folks together, and she started singing while I accompanied her on the piano. We worked real well together, and so one thing sort of led to the other. You know how it is."

"I hope the two of you will be very happy together. When's the wedding?"

"We figured that maybe we'd get hitched next month before it gets too hot down here. We'd both really like it if you could come down for the ceremony. I want you to meet Gina, and you've never seen my setup down here. It's really pretty sweet."

"You set the date, and I'll be there."

"If you want to bring a date along with you, feel free."

"I'll see."

Her father was silent for a moment. "I know that John's death hit you hard, but it's been almost two years now. Maybe it's time to start getting on with your life."

"You could be right," she said in a tone that didn't encourage further discussion.

"Another thing. Would you tell your Uncle Harold about this? I know I should call him myself, but I'm afraid that he'll just make me feel guilty. Even if he doesn't say anything, I'll be able to tell by the tone of his voice that he'll never forgive me for replacing Miriam. He always thought that he loved her more than I did, and this will just prove it to him. Now he can go on grieving for her long after I've remarried."

"I wouldn't be so sure of that," Summyr said, and told him about Harold's girlfriend.

A loud laugh came down the line. "Why the old dog! He spent the first half of his life wishing he'd married your mother. I thought for sure he'd spend the rest of his life mourning for her. This Babe must be quite a woman to get Harold out of his bachelor ways."

"I guess."

"Well, maybe you could still break the news to him. Then if he takes it okay, I'll invite him and his woman to my wedding. How does that sound?"

"Sounds great," Summyr agreed.

No sooner had Summyr hung up the phone than it rang again. Surely this time it would be Steve.

"Hello, Summyr," Uncle Harold said. "Have you eaten yet?"

"No, I just got in."

"Would you like to come over to my house? Babe is here for dinner, and she'd like to meet you."

A woman's voice said something in the background, and Uncle Harold covered the phone for a moment.

There was laughter in the background when he came back on the line. "How about seven?"

It had been a long hard day, and the last thing she wanted to do was be on her best behavior with Uncle Harold's new friend. But a refusal could be seen as some kind of negative judgment, and a Saturday night out, even with relatives, was better than one spent watching television and wondering why Steve didn't call. Plus it would give her a chance to see her uncle's face when she broke the news of her father's impending marriage. That way she'd be better able to judge whether he'd be disposed to make the trip to Florida. It would also be an opportunity to form an opinion of Babe. Plus, her uncle liked his meat, and a good piece of beef would hit the spot about now.

But what if I don't like her? Or, worse yet, what if I think she's bad for Uncle Harold? What will I do then? Pushing those thoughts aside, she said, "I'll be there at seven."

"Wonderful." Uncle Harold lowered his voice. "I'm really looking forward to your meeting Babe."

"Yes. So am I," Summyr said, trying to keep even the hint of a doubt from her voice.

After speaking with her uncle, Summyr decided that a shower would be a good idea. It would help her to relax and get into the proper frame of mind to greet a potential candidate for "aunt." Getting out of her yoga clothes and tossing them into the hamper, she turned the water on as hot as she could stand and stepped into the shower. Slowly the knotted muscles in her neck and shoulders began to loosen as the water streamed over her body, and as she washed her hair, letting the water run over her head for a long time, even the tension in her mind began to slowly unwind.

I really have only two problems, Summyr reasoned. How to keep the yoga studio open. And whether to keep seeing Steve. Reducing the number of concerns to two big ones somehow made her feel better, even though each of those problems quickly gave birth to a number of others. Where would she find a new place for the studio? How could she find a new job to help support it? Why hadn't Steve called her back? What would she do if it turned out that he had flagrantly lied to her?

Sighing, she stepped out of the shower and vigorously rubbed herself dry. She decided to wear a pink oxford shirt and tan chinos, a casual look that she made a bit more formal by adding a blue linen blazer. Summyr looked in the mirror as she went out the door and decided that she looked just right for the role of the concerned niece who is interviewing her bachelor uncle's girlfriend.

She took her time driving to her uncle's, consciously making an effort to put her own problems out of her mind. One thing yoga had taught her was that worrying is a needless waste of energy. Constructive planning was one thing, but simply dwelling on one's fears, letting them circle around and around in your mind like endless reruns of a bad television show, was not productive. That made everything seem worse, and did nothing to assist in arriving at a solution.

Her mind was almost serene by the time she rang the bell at her uncle's house. The door quickly opened, and her uncle stood there beaming at her.

"Come in, come in," he said, taking her elbow and urging her into the living room on the right.

When Summyr entered the room, with her uncle standing just behind her and gently pushing her forward, the first thing she saw was Janet Benson sitting on the sofa looking more grim than she normally did.

"Hi, what a surprise seeing you here," Summyr said,

her eyes still surveying the room for the notorious Babe. She was a bit surprised that her uncle even knew Janet, and wondered why he had invited her over for this family occasion.

Her uncle darted around in front of her. "Summyr," he said, delight evident in his voice, "I'd like you to meet Babe Benson."

Automatically Summyr stepped forward and put out her hand as Janet stood up. Even as she did so, Summyr felt a bit silly at being so formal with someone whose body she had tugged and pulled on for several months, but she was so stunned that she didn't know what else to do. Janet ignored the offered hand and enveloped Summyr in a giant hug.

"I'm sorry to shock you," Janet said. "Harold thought it would be fun to surprise you. I wasn't sure it was such a good idea."

Her uncle laughed a bit nervously. "It was just that you've been so obviously concerned about my new girlfriend that I thought it would be a pleasant surprise for you to find out that it was someone you already knew and liked."

Summyr sank down on the sofa next to Janet.

"Well, it certainly was a surprise."

Janet patted her knee. "I told your uncle that we should have let you know right away that he was going out with someone you knew."

"Why didn't you tell me the other day when you first met my uncle?"

Janet looked down at the rug and gave an embarrassed smile. "To be honest, Summyr, I never knew your last name. You know how it is at the yoga studio, everyone is on a first-name basis. I just made out my check to the studio name. I'm sure you must have told me your last name when I first joined, but it never registered with me at the time. So when I came to your uncle for legal advice on purchasing a building, I never realized the two of you were related. I only discovered it last night when we went out, and he began telling me about his niece the yoga instructor."

"And that's when you decided to keep me in the dark?" Summyr said, looking at her uncle.

"You were giving me such a hard time about going out with someone that I thought it would be best to show you in a dramatic way that your concerns were unnecessary." He paused to clear his throat. "Now that I think about it, it was a rather thoughtless prank. I find that recently I am given to being a bit more boyish that normal."

His look of contrition was so sincere that Summyr smiled.

"Well, I guess there was no harm done except for taking a year or two off of my life when I walked in the room. Is Babe actually your nickname?"

Janet nodded. "Ever since I was a child. I don't tell everyone, only people that I get close to."

She smiled at Summyr's uncle, who excused himself and disappeared into the kitchen where he said that he was preparing a culinary feast.

"You met my uncle when you went to him for legal help in purchasing that building in the center of town where the dance studio used to be."

Janet nodded. "My late husband, Frank, left me with lots of money and not much to do. My two sons are grown, and for the last year or so I've spent my time adjusting to being alone and wondering what I would do with the rest of my life. The other day when we talked about Chrissy and what she needed in her life, the idea just came to me that maybe the solution to Chrissy's problem could also be the solution to mine. If I bought that building, I could turn that old shop into an organic food store."

"So you and Chrissy would work together?"

"Not all the time. I'd like to work there a couple of days a week. But I want to travel, and now that I've met Harold, well, who knows. But it's always good for a person to have some kind of a job to keep them grounded. But Chrissy would be the boss. I'll be a silent partner—at least as silent as I can be."

"Do you know that Chrissy quit Root and Branch today?"

Janet nodded. "She called me from home early this afternoon. I can't believe the nerve of that Richie. She should have quit that place a long time ago. I told Chrissy that I'll start paying her salary next week. We have to begin making plans for the store, the closing on the building is in two weeks. I'd like us to be up and running by the Fourth of July at the latest."

"I think what you're doing for Chrissy is really great. Not just with the store, but helping her improve her appearance."

"There's still a ways to go there. But as she gets happier with her life, I think she'll start to take more pride in her appearance. She's a wonderful girl. I just want her to be confident enough to show that to the world."

"If the way she stood up to Richie today is any indication, I'd say that she's already on the road to an improved self-image."

Janet nodded, then she looked across the room as though trying to decide how to broach a difficult subject.

"I know that I can be kind of bossy sometimes, especially with young women. I guess I always would have liked to have had a daughter, and when I see someone who fits into that age-group, I sometimes can't helping giving an overabundance of good advice."

"I think you've done just fine with Chrissy," Summyr assured her.

"Yes, well, it wasn't Chrissy that I was talking about. It was you."

"Oh?"

"Harold told me that you were interested in the space that the dance studio formerly occupied, and I'd certainly like to rent it to you at a low rate. But I don't think that would really be the solution to your problems."

Summyr gave her a quizzical look but remained silent.

"Look, don't get me wrong; I know you aren't Chrissy. You're a strong, independent young woman," Janet said, reaching over to put a hand on Summyr's arm. "But I think you've got yourself in what my late husband would call 'an untenable business situation.' "

"Is that like being on the verge of bankruptcy?" Summyr said with a small smile.

"Let's just say that you're undercapitalized. You don't have the money to concentrate on just running the yoga studio, so you have to spend half your time working at something else. That means the yoga studio never quite gets off the ground, so you have to keep a part-time job. It's a vicious cycle."

"I can't disagree with that."

"My proposal is that you let me become a partner with you in the yoga studio."

Summyr frowned. The studio was hers. She had built it up to what it was. Even if that didn't make it quite viable, she wasn't about to turn it over to someone else.

Janet seemed to read her mind. "You would have the controlling interest. Let's say we split sixty-forty. You own sixty percent. In exchange for my forty percent, I'll fix up the old dance studio and rent it to us at the same rent you're paying now. In addition, I'll throw in some money for advertising."

"That sounds fine," Summyr said cautiously. "But I'll still have the same problem holding down a part-time job. How will I be able to expand the class schedule?"

"You think that you need to offer more evening classes, right?"

Summyr nodded.

"I've already discussed this with Chrissy, and we

were wondering if you'd be interested in working in the new store some mornings and some afternoons. That way you could have the evenings free to offer yoga classes. You could still offer some morning and evening classes—after all, the studio will only be one flight up from the store."

"Are you sure that you'll really need me in the store? I know that making a go of the store is important to you and Chrissy, and I wouldn't want to be taking charity."

"There's no charity involved," Janet said firmly. "Chrissy will be the manager, and I'll only drop in to work a few times a week. She'll need experienced, reliable part-time help. You're perfect."

"Well, if you're sure that you can really use me, I'll be happy to work in the new store."

Janet's face broke out in a smile, and she scooted along the sofa to give Summyr a hug. "And I want you to go on the payroll next week as well. You can divide your time between helping Chrissy set up plans for the store, and helping me decided how to renovate the old dance space."

"The only problem is that I have to be out of the warehouse by the end of the month, and we probably won't be able to open in the new space for another couple of months. If I'm closed for that long, I could lose some of the students that I already have."

"Hmm. Let's think about that for a while. Maybe we can come up with some alternative until the new studio is open." Janet dropped her voice down to a whisper. "I also want you to know that this is a business deal, and it has nothing to do with my relationship with your uncle. Things are going great right now, and I don't see any clouds on the horizon. But I want you to know that I keep my business and my personal life separate."

"What? Are you two women already whispering together? Can't I leave you alone for a few minutes without a conspiracy of some sort developing?" Harold asked, coming into the room and putting his hands on Janet's shoulders.

His expression was so content that Summyr had to smile. Gone was the heartbreaking look of loneliness that had crept over his face when he thought no one was looking ever since Summyr's mother had died. Summyr found herself devoutly hoping that his relationship with Janet would be a lifelong one. The idea of a lifelong relationship brought to mind her father's plans.

"I got a call from Dad today. He's getting married."

A brief look of surprise passed over Harold's face, then he smiled. "That's good. Sam couldn't have been happy living alone, and I'm sure that Miriam wouldn't have expected it."

"Well, if you can find the time, we've all been invited to the wedding next month."

"Would you like to take a short vacation in Florida, Babe?" Uncle Harold asked.

"I'm sure I can squeeze it in along with everything else. One of my sons lives down there, too, so maybe we can work in a visit to both of our families."

"Good," said Harold. "And now the time has come to partake in our special evening meal."

They went into the dining room and sat down: Janet and Harold at either end of the table, for all the world like they were husband and wife. Summyr took her place to her uncle's right, thinking that his relationship with Janet showed every sign of turning into something permanent.

Her uncle reached over and dramatically lifted the lid on a covered platter in the middle of the table.

"This is especially for you!"

Summyr stared at the brownish loaf that filled the center of the platter.

"What is it?" she asked politely.

"Sweet potato, oatmeal, and cashew loaf," Janet said.

"I know how you try to eat vegetarian most of the time, and since Babe will be going into the health-food business, we thought it would be a good idea to start off on the right foot," Harold said, beaming at her.

"Well, thank you for thinking about me," Summyr said, her vision of prime rib fading into the distance.

Her uncle disappeared into the kitchen. "And to go along with it," he said, returning to the dining room with his hands full, "we have a nice big salad and a bowl of steamed broccoli."

"Wonderful," Summyr said weakly.

"Should we tell her about the surprise we're having for dessert?" Harold asked, looking at Janet.

"Well, now that you've mentioned it, we shouldn't keep the poor girl in suspense," Janet replied.

"I've heard that it's the food of the future," Uncle Harold said. "So it's something special that I made myself."

"What are we having?" Summyr asked with a sense of foreboding.

Her uncle beamed proudly. "Tofu rice pudding."

When the meal was over, Summyr had to admit that it had tasted better than she would have expected on sight. Of course, that was usually the way with vegetarian dishes, which tended to appear rather plain, but often were more flavorful than expected. Covered with a nice peanut sauce, the loaf had proved remarkably good, and although a bit filling as a dessert, the tofu rice pudding also tasted very much like the real thing. When the last spoon had finished rattling around in a pudding dish, all three, by a sort of unspoken consent, looked around the table at each other and smiled.

"An excellent meal, Uncle Harold," Summyr said.

He grinned modestly. "I had Janet's help with the loaf. Grinding up all the cashews was quite a chore."

"I enjoyed helping," Janet said. "One of the things I like least about being alone is not having someone else to cook for. It's hard to work up much enthusiasm for meals when you're going to be eating the food by yourself."

Summyr agreed. Although she tried to pay attention to her diet and prepare a good homemade meal for herself every day, it was difficult to make an effort when you were only cooking for one. The most fun she'd had cooking recently had been on the day that Steve had been over for dinner. Thinking of Steve made her frown.

"What's the matter?" Janet asked.

Summyr shook her head. Since her mother died, she'd handled relationship problems by herself, and Summyr wasn't sure that she wanted that to change.

"Is there a problem with Steve?" Janet asked.

Summyr's eyes opened in surprise.

"Who's Steve?" Uncle Harold asked, a confused expression on his face, as if he'd dozed off for a second and the conversation had gotten completely away from him.

"A good friend of Summyr's. At least I think he's a good friend." Janet looked at her questioningly.

Summyr frowned. "I'm not sure what the answer is to that myself."

"Would you like to talk about it?" asked Janet.

"Let me go out in the kitchen and start cleaning up," Uncle Harold said, quickly starting to stack the dessert dishes.

"You can stay," said Summyr.

"No, that's quite all right. I've always felt that there are some conversations that women should have between themselves. The same holds true of men."

When Harold had cleared the table and could be heard putting the dishes in the dishwasher, Janet said, "You don't have to tell me anything either. I don't mean to pry."

"That's okay," Summyr said, and she realized that

she actually would like to talk to another woman about the situation. Summyr told Janet about her discovery of Steve's profession and of how he had lied to her.

"I see," Janet said after Summyr had concluded. "Do you have any idea why he didn't tell you he was a police officer?"

Summyr shrugged. "Maybe because I made it pretty clear to him that I planned to avoid men who took a lot of risks."

"So he lied because he thought that otherwise you wouldn't go out with him?"

"I suppose. I can't think of another reason."

"You must have made it very clear that you weren't about to make any exceptions."

Summyr smiled. "I guess I did come on a little strong about it. But he got me talking about John and his mountain climbing."

"I see. Your uncle told me about what happened there. I'm sorry."

"I still get pretty excited when I talk about it, so it probably seemed to Steve that if he told me he was anything as dangerous as a cop I'd run out of the room screaming."

"And would you have refused to go out with him if you'd known what he did?" asked Janet.

Summyr paused. That was a question she hadn't fully considered.

"A few days ago, I'd have said yes, but now I don't know. I've been thinking a lot lately about why I loved John, and I've come to believe that at least part of his attraction for me was that he had an adventurous side to him. I used to think that I loved him because he was gentle, stable, and would have been a good family man. But now I'm starting to wonder if the mountain climbing part of his personality didn't have some appeal to me as well."

Janet nodded. "It's hard to know sometimes what makes one person appeal to us while another one doesn't. My late husband wasn't a very handsome man, and he certainly wasn't rich when I married him. But he was one of the most exciting men that I've ever met. He always had a plan. When we first met he had just decided to open a string of laundromats, which doesn't sound very exciting, I guess, but he made it seem like the biggest adventure on earth. Where to put them, how to maintain them, what equipment to buy, he threw himself into those questions with a passion."

"Was he successful?"

"Oh, yes. Within five years he was franchising them out all over the city, and when he sold the company a few years later to move into computer sales, he was a millionaire. I think it was the way he put his whole heart into everything he did that made him so appealing to me. I've never had much time for people who nibble around the edges of life. 'Take a big bite and see how much you can chew.' That's always been my motto."

"But all the same, Steve did lie to me."

Janet looked thoughtful. "Lying is something I never could abide either. But before you judge him, I think you have to find out why he lied. Maybe there's no more to it than you've figured out."

"Do you think so?" Summyr asked hopefully.

"It's possible. All I'm saying is that you should give him a chance to explain."

"All right," Summyr agreed. "I will. I do like being with him. He's funny and nice, but at the same time kind of exciting."

"And he's certainly handsome," Janet added with a grin.

"Let me ask you one more question," said Summyr. "What is it about Uncle Harold that you find so appealing?"

"That's easy. Have you ever met another man who could stay in love for over thirty years with a woman he hadn't touched and who was married to someone else? I tell you, Summyr, that's the kind of passion you don't see every day. Harold seems quiet and a little bland, but you know what they say about still waters?"

"They run deep."

Janet winked. "Now let's go out in the kitchen and let Harold know that we're done. Otherwise he'll move on to mopping the kitchen floor."

When Summyr returned home that night, she checked her answering machine, but there was no message from Steve. I want to give him a chance, Summyr thought, as she got ready for bed, but he's got to call and explain. He owes me at least that much. She lay awake for a long while, half-hoping that she'd receive a late call, and half-wondering what she would do if she did.

Chapter Fourteen

By the time the afternoon of the next day, which was Sunday, had rolled around without a word from Steve, Summyr had reached the limit of her tolerance. She had cleaned the apartment within an inch of its life, cooked herself a scrumptious dinner then left most of it uneaten, and read the newspaper from front to back. Finally she decided that there was no point in slavishly remaining in the apartment so she could catch Steve's call as soon as it came in. Her machine would pick up any messages, and it would serve him right for making her wait so long.

She threw on a jacket, went downstairs, and got in her car. Then she sat there wondering where in the world she should go. She'd just been to Uncle Harold's last night and, anyway, he had said something about going to a museum with Janet this afternoon.

She could swing by Chrissy's house and see if she wanted to go do something. But Chrissy would ask about Steve, and Summyr didn't want to explain the situation all over again. She had a number of other friends in town, but none that she knew well enough to drop in on without calling first. And, she thought, I'm probably not going to be very good company right now. With a sigh, she finally pulled out of the parking lot and headed for the yoga studio. Maybe doing some yoga and a bit of meditation would relax her mind.

The streets of Eastfield were as deserted as usual on a Sunday, and the neighborhood around the warehouse, being largely commercial, was completely abandoned. Summyr went upstairs to the studio, her mind preoccupied with thoughts of Steve. Only when she reached the landing did she notice that the door to the studio was wide open. *Schuster again!* Even with a broken leg, he was back sneaking around the studio. She angrily marched into the studio, ready to have it out with him once and for all for invading her space without permission.

Not even bothering to take off her shoes, she walked through the vestibule and into the center of the studio. She stopped. There was no one there. Stunned, she stood there, foolishly looking around as if the fat little man could be hiding behind a pillow or a pile of blankets. She spotted an aluminum ladder leaning against the wall. Could that be hers? But surely that was locked in the closet. She eyed the door to the closet. Could he have taken out the ladder and be hiding in there now? But she always kept it locked because the door didn't shut right. Then she heard the studio door swing closed. She rushed out into the vestibule, hoping to catch him before he escaped, but as she went through the door from the studio, someone shoved her hard from behind and sent her sprawling across her desk.

She lay there for a moment across the desk, surprised and trying to register what had happened. Then she stood up straight and turned around.

"Don't do anything stupid," Alicia said. She stood between Summyr and the doorway. In her right hand she held a crowbar.

"What are you doing here, Alicia?" Summyr said, confusion more than anger in her voice. "How did you get in?"

Alicia looked in the direction of the door. Summyr could see now that the frame had been splintered where Alicia had pried the door open. If I hadn't been in such a hurry to bawl Schuster out, I'd have noticed that, thought Summyr, and I never would have come inside.

"Sorry about the door. I tried to steal your keys the other day so I could make a copy, but you came along and helpfully showed me the box where I could put my payment." Alicia smiled slightly. "Actually, you've made this whole thing hard for me. You even closed the window I opened the other night to climb into the warehouse. This time I was smarter and just left the window unlocked and shoved it open from the outside when I got here today."

"But why? I don't have anything worth stealing."

"I'm not going to take anything of yours. I'm just getting back some property of mine."

"What are you talking about?"

"You don't need to know. All you need to remember is that if you don't give me any trouble, you won't get hurt."

Summyr estimated the distance to the door.

"Don't try it," Alicia warned, tapping the crowbar in her palm. "I don't want to hurt you. But I need some time, and you'd run right to the police."

Summyr was a couple of inches taller than Alicia, but Alicia was strong and the crowbar gave her a decisive edge. The hard look in her eye suggested that she wouldn't hesitate to use it.

"Where do you keep the key to the closet?" Alicia asked.

"I don't have one."

"Don't lie. I've seen you unlock the closet and take out a vacuum cleaner after class."

"It's on the hook behind the desk," Summyr said.

"Get it."

Summyr slowly went behind the desk, scanning its surface for something she might use as a weapon. Papers, pens, and a couple of books, nothing that would help her match up against a strong young woman with a crowbar. She took the key off the hook.

"Throw it to me."

Summyr tossed the key to Alicia, who easily caught it in one hand.

"Now go back in the studio."

Summyr walked into the studio with Alicia a few

steps behind her, far enough away that Summyr couldn't try any tricks, but close enough to use the crowbar if necessary.

"Go over to the closet."

Summyr obeyed.

"Stand to one side of the door."

As Summyr stood next to the closet door, Alicia, not taking her eyes off Summyr for a second, opened the door with one hand. Summyr considered whether she could dart around the other woman and make it out of the studio. There was a slim chance. But a quick swing of the crowbar to a shin or knee would easily bring her down, and she knew from watching Alicia in yoga that she had the grace and speed of an athlete.

"Get inside," Alicia ordered.

Summyr looked in the darkness. "Couldn't we talk about this?"

"No."

Summyr walked into the darkness and the door shut behind her. She heard the key turn.

"Now be quiet and nothing will happen to you," Alicia said.

"How am I going to get out of here?" Summyr asked. If she was left in the closet there was no telling when she would be found. No one else came into the studio except for her, so who would notice she was missing? If she didn't appear, her students would simply assume that she had cancelled class due to an emergency. No one would notify the police. Maybe after a couple of days of not hearing from her, Chrissy or Uncle Harold would wonder where she was. But how long would it take them to think to check the yoga studio? She banged hard on the door. "You have to let me out. No one will know I'm here."

"I'll let you out before I leave," Alicia said. "Now be quiet."

Summyr wanted to keep talking to Alicia. Anything to keep in contact with the world outside of the closet. But she knew that there was nothing she could say that would get Alicia to release her, and there was no point in annoying her and risking a blow from the crowbar. She walked to the back of the closet and found the vacuum cleaner. She grabbed its handle, strangely comforted by the feel of something familiar. Summyr stood there listening carefully to see if she could detect what was going on in the outer room.

She soon heard a great deal of noise. It sounded as if it were coming from overhead. After a few seconds, Summyr figured out that Alicia was doing something to the ceiling, and the sound was reverberating all along the dead air space between the ceiling and the roof. Although she couldn't be certain, it sounded as if Alicia was tearing down the acoustical tiles. Summyr thought back to when she had found Schuster—he had also been taking down tiles to examine the ceiling. Maybe his fall had been no accident.

Deciding that the more she stood there doing nothing the more panicked she would become, Summyr began feeling her way around the closet. She soon discovered the aluminum ladder back in the corner behind the vacuum. That meant that Alicia had brought one of her own. Summyr also found the broom she used to sweep the tile floor in the office. She paused for a moment when she found the broom. What if she created such a commotion that Alicia opened the door? Could she charge out with the broom in front of her and catch Alicia off guard? She tried to imagine the encounter and decided that the crowbar might easily beat out the broom.

At the end of her circuit of the closet her hands found a switch next to the doorway. Smiling at her own ignorance, she flipped the switch and the closet was flooded with light from one dim bulb. I never even noticed that there was a light in the closet, she thought. Every time I've used the closet it's been daylight or the lights in the studio have been on. I should have guessed that a business office wouldn't have had a closet without lights. Unfortunately, the light didn't reveal any useful implements that would help her to escape or to defend herself. A few dust cloths on the floor and a bucket with some cleaning supplies were all she had missed.

The tile removal was coming closer, making the ceiling above her head rattle. Summyr looked up. The tiles there were the same as in the studio: acoustical rectangles about three feet by two feet. As she stood staring at the ceiling, a plan began to form. She studied the door frame. The top of the frame seemed to stop at the ceiling. Could it be that there was space above the door lintel, so if she climbed up into the crawl space between the ceiling and the roof, she could come down on the outside of the closet?

Summyr got her ladder out from behind the vacuum

cleaner and set it up under the tile closest to the door. She climbed up the steps until she was in position to push firmly on the tile above her head. She placed both hands flat on the tile and shoved. Nothing happened. *Could something have been used to secure it in place?* she thought, disappointment washing over her. *But why would this one be screwed or nailed down if none of the others were?* She pushed harder and felt the tile begin to move. Gradually it went up about two inches, and she slowly began sliding it out of the frame. Just when she thought it was sliding out of the way, it tilted as if something heavy was weighing down one end. Something heavy dropped out of the space, just barely missing her face. It bounced hard off her shoulder and banged off the ladder before landing on the floor.

Summyr froze, waiting to see if Alicia would come to investigate. There seemed to be a momentary pause on the other end of the room, as if Alicia was wondering if she had heard something. Then, apparently satisfied that nothing important had happened, she returned to work. Summyr scrambled down the ladder and examined the object. It was a metal box. She estimated that it was a little over a foot long, about ten inches wide and six inches deep. Summyr tried to open it, but it was locked.

This is probably what Alicia is looking for, Summyr thought, should I tell her that I have it? Maybe she'll let me out of the closet and then go on her way. As much as Summyr wanted that simple solution to be true, she couldn't convince herself of it. *Alicia will take the box, all right, but there's no way she's going*

*to let me out of the closet to go to the police. No, an
essential part of Alicia's plan is leaving me in here
until she's had plenty of time to leave town.*

Climbing up the ladder again and placing the box
on the paint platform, Summyr stuck her head up into
the space between the ceiling and the roof. About
twenty-five feet to her right, daylight poured through
the spaces where Alicia had removed the tiles. She
was still working feverishly, but fortunately her back
was to Summyr. Going up one step above what was
safely recommended, Summyr began to gently remove
the tile on the other side of the closet door, hoping
that the damage Schuster had done to the ladder
wouldn't bring her tumbling down. Keeping one eye
on Alicia, Summyr tried to time her movements with
the other woman's so no sounds would give her away.
Soon she had the other tile out of the way and could
see down to the floor on the outside of the closet.

Now came the hard part. She would have to step
off the ladder, straddle the lintel of the closet door,
then lower herself down to the floor; all without alert-
ing Alicia who was coming closer with every tile she
removed. That would be relatively easy to do if she
left the box in the closet, but Summyr didn't want to
take the risk that Alicia would find it and make her
escape before Summyr could bring the police. Locking
her in the closet had made this a personal matter, and
Summyr was determined to prevent Alicia from getting the box.

Summyr carefully put one leg across the top of the
doorframe with the other leg still in the closet. Tuck-

ing the box under her left arm, she grabbed the top of
the frame with her right hand and then swung her right
leg over. She hung for a moment outside the closet
door, her feet dangling three feet above the floor and
her shoulder joint making an ominous popping sound.
Thankful that she wasn't any heavier or any shorter,
she let go. The impact when she hit the floor went up
her feet and through her knees like an electric shock.
She staggered backwards and lost her balance. Summyr reached back with her left hand to keep from falling, and the box fell from under her arm onto the floor,
bouncing off the wall on the way down.

She was on her feet in an instant, then staggered as
her right ankle gave way under her. She grabbed the
box and began limping towards the door, but Alicia
had heard the noise and come down the ladder as
quick as a cat.

"Where do you think you're going with that?" she
asked.

Summyr remained silent, trying to calculate her
chances of reaching the door. Alicia had the crowbar
in her hand. She also had the better angle and would
reach the door a step ahead of Summyr, especially
given the bad ankle.

"Throw the box over here, and I'll let you go," Alicia said softly.

Summyr nodded and pretended to reach back to toss
her the box. Then she sprinted for the door, trying to
ignore the pain in her ankle. Alicia muttered a curse
and ran after her. Summyr could feel Alicia's hand
grab her shirt as she reached the office, so without

stopping she threw the box across the room and through the front office window. Whether it was the loud shattering of glass or seeing the box suddenly separated from the person she was following, Alicia hesitated for an instant, giving Summyr just enough time to pull away and dart through the doorway. But Summyr could hear Alicia pounding down the stairs right behind her. She tore through the door to the warehouse and out into the daylight, struggling to get her car keys out of her pocket, hoping that Alicia would go for the box first and give her time to escape.

But Alicia wasn't going to make the same mistake twice. She caught up with Summyr just as Summyr was trying to put the key in the car door, twisted her around, and pushed her against the side of the car. Summyr struggled, trying to break free, as Alicia began to raise her hand holding the crowbar. Suddenly, Alicia let out a grunt of surprise and pain as her arms were twisted behind her.

"I don't think you want to do that," Steve said, quickly handcuffing her wrists. Alicia struggled and tried to run away, but Steve wrestled her into the open door of the backseat of his car. He shut the door and electronically locked it.

In the distance, Summyr heard sirens.

"Good, help is on the way," Steve said, putting an arm around her as her knees began to tremble and she started to collapse.

He quickly took the keys from her hand and opened her car door.

"Why don't you sit down and rest for a while?"

Summyr tried to speak, but she found that a nod was about all she could manage. Steve walked over to the sidewalk in front of the building and picked up the box.

"Did you throw this out the window?"

Summyr tried another nod.

Steve smiled. "You almost hit me on the head."

"I wasn't trying to."

Steve's expression turned serious. "I wouldn't really blame you if you were. I'm going to explain things a little later and hope that you'll try to forgive me."

"Good." That seems like the appropriate word, she thought slowly, it doesn't commit me to much.

Steve smiled again. "You must have a lot of money."

She tried to ask why, but all she could manage was a puzzled expression.

"Because you just threw a hundred thousand dollars out the window."

Summyr leaned her head back against the car seat and closed her eyes.

Chapter Fifteen

Summyr sat over the cup of coffee and inhaled the rich fragrance. Uncle Harold watched her carefully from the other end of the dining room table.

"Is it too strong for you? Would you rather have some herbal tea?" he asked anxiously.

She shook her head. "No, I think this is just what I need right now," Summyr said, taking a sip.

"Are you sure that all you want is toast?"

"For right now," she replied, looking at the plate piled high with several kinds of toast that her uncle had placed at her end of the table. Butter, magarine, several jams and jellies, and even peanut butter stood nearby.

She slowly buttered a piece of whole wheat toast and had begun to chew when the doorbell rang.

"Do you want me to have him wait in the living room while you eat?"

Summyr shook her head.

"Would you like me to be with you?" Uncle Harold said, walking down to her end of the table and standing next to her.

Summyr reached out and took his hand. "You're being awfully sweet, Uncle Harold, but I can handle this by myself."

Her uncle smiled. "That's the trouble with young women today, they're so strong and independent that they don't give their uncles a chance to spoil them."

"I'll give you plenty of opportunity to do that when this is all over with. I promise," Summyr said.

Nodding, Uncle Harold left to answer the door. A few minutes later, Steve entered the dining room alone.

"So how is the heroine of the hour?" he asked, sitting down next to her. "How's the ankle?"

"The doctor said it was a sprain. I've got it taped. It should be fine in a couple of weeks. Otherwise, I'm sore, irritable, curious, and still a bit queasy. It's not every day that someone tries to brain me with a tire iron."

"Yes. You'd have hoped that Alicia would have had more of that gentle yogic spirit," Steve said with a smile.

"Okay," Summyr said briskly, suddenly tired of the give-and-take, "I've tried to act brave and you've tried to act funny. Can we get to the facts? What was this all about?"

The smile disappeared from Steve's face.

"Do you remember when I was over at your place for dinner, and I mentioned that your studio is in the warehouse where Consolidated Trucking used to be?"

Summyr nodded.

"And you said that the company went out of business when a bookkeeper embezzled funds."

"That's what I seem to remember."

"Well, you're right. Three years ago the guy in charge of keeping the books was found guilty of stealing money from the company. He had set up a series of false accounts and made up bills in their names. Then he paid money into these phony accounts, and later took the money out of the accounts for himself. It came to around one hundred thousand. He got caught because the owner wondered why the company was losing money and secretly brought in an outside auditor."

"Were you involved in catching him?"

"No. I was on the Springfield force. I only came into the picture recently."

Summyr noticed his use of the word 'was' but said nothing.

"This bookkeeper, his name is Peterson, was convicted and sent to jail for five years. But what made the case interesting is that the money he embezzled was never found. The phony accounts had been emptied out by Peterson a few days before he was arrested, but the money wasn't in his apartment. And there were no records of where he might have stashed it. The district attorney even offered to give him a lighter sentence in return for the money, but he refused."

"Was Alicia somehow involved in all this?"

Steve nodded. "Up to her neck. She was a secretary at the trucking company. Peterson wouldn't say anything to implicate her, but some of the other employees said that the two of them had been going out together. They even suspected that Alicia was the one who put him up to it. Peterson comes across as kind of a weak guy, so it's possible that Alicia talked him into the whole thing. But we never had enough evidence to charge her."

"So three years ago Peterson went to jail. Then Consolidated Trucking went out of business."

"Yeah. They hadn't been doing real well, and the loss of all that money came at a bad time. The owner of the company even hired a friend of mine who works as a private investigator specializing in financial fraud to see if he could find the money. But he had no luck. My friend, however, made a deal with a prison guard to keep track of all Peterson's visitors. And about three months ago, Alicia came to visit him for the first time."

"Was she still living around here?" asked Summyr.

"No. Before Peterson's conviction, she moved to Boston and got another secretarial job. After meeting with Peterson in prison three months ago, however, she left Boston, moved back here, and started showing up at your yoga classes. My friend figured that Peterson must have told her generally where the money was. Peterson was going to get two years off for good behavior, so he probably figured that when he got out in four months, they'd get the money together. Then he and Alicia could take off and start living the good life."

"Couldn't Alicia just have taken the money and disappeared without him?"

"If she could find it, but that involved tearing down the entire ceiling. Apparently she decided that the risk was worth it if it meant she wouldn't have to share with Peterson."

"Peterson was pretty gullible."

"He probably thought that Alicia cared for him, and he never guessed that she would go to such extremes to find the money. But he might have had some second thoughts because he put his sister's husband on the case as well."

"Who was that?"

"Louie Schuster, our roving contractor. He visited Peterson in prison, and the timing couldn't have been better because the owners of the warehouse had just decided to renovate the building. Schuster told them he wanted to inspect the building before making a bid. He got the keys and then started searching for the money."

"But apparently Peterson didn't trust him much more than Alicia," said Summyr, "because he was looking in the wrong spot as well."

"The closet threw him off. I talked to the guy who used to own Consolidated. They added that closet after Peterson went to prison. That changed the layout of the room and confused Schuster. Then once he broke his leg that left a clear field for Alicia."

"Why was he downstairs in the warehouse when we first saw him?"

"Probably he wanted to rig the window so he could get back in any time he wanted in case the search took a while. Pretty much the same idea that Alicia had."

"Then he fell off my ladder and broke his leg."

"Fell or was pushed. My friend and I have been keeping Alicia under surveillance almost around the clock, but she got away from us a couple of times. Unfortunately, my friend is better at crunching numbers than tailing someone. That morning when Schuster fell, she was out, and we don't know where she went."

"Wouldn't Schuster know?"

"If he had his head up above the tiles, he'd never have seen her. And even if he did know that she was the one who pushed him off the ladder, he's not likely to want to get involved in a criminal proceeding. But we've got her for the attempted assault on you, and breaking and entering. Most important of all, she didn't get the money, so that can go back to the company it was embezzled from."

Summyr paused, aware that the rest of her questions were going to cut closer to the bone of their relationship.

"Why didn't you tell me you were a police officer?"

Steve paused. "When I first came to the yoga studio, I was there mainly to keep an eye on Alicia. My friend and I had a suspicion that Peterson had told her where the money was, and when she suddenly returned to Eastfield and started taking classes in the old warehouse, we figured that Peterson must have hidden the money right at his place of employment. After all, when you think about it, that was the perfect spot. No one would ever look there."

"You could still have told me who you were."

"I was undercover. After all, I couldn't have you telling Alicia that I was a cop."

"I wouldn't have done that if you'd explained everything to me."

"I didn't know that when we first met."

"What about later?"

Steve looked across the room. "Okay, I'll admit that when you told me about how you wanted someone who was stable and how your fiancé had let you down by dying in a mountain climbing accident, I figured that if I told you I was a cop you wouldn't want to see me anymore."

"So you lied about working for a drug company? Did you lie about having an injured shoulder as well?" Summyr asked, her lips forming a tight line.

Steve shook his head and smiled slightly. "The shoulder is one point in my favor. I really did have surgery on it. It happened pretty much as I told you, only I was in a police cruiser chasing a drunk at the time when he turned around and came right at me."

"And what about your imaginary job?"

"Yeah. Well, I guess I did make up most of that. Actually a cousin of mine wanted me to go into that.

He told me all about it. I've been giving it some thought."

"You're thinking about leaving the police?"

Steve shrugged "This shoulder will never be completely right. The police doctor will probably have me put on restricted duty for an indefinite period. Sitting behind a desk or going around to schools telling kids why they should stay off drugs isn't what I joined the force to do. Don't get me wrong, it's worthwhile work, but that's for a guy at the end of his career, not for me."

"But selling pharmaceuticals," said Summyr. "That seems like such . . ."

"A big change. Yeah, I know. I was having a lot of trouble adjusting to the idea myself," Steve said with a grin, then his expression turned contrite. "I guess what I lied about the most to you was in pretending to be someone who doesn't like to take risks. There is a part of me that enjoys adventure, the thrill of catching the bad guys."

"And you didn't think that I could accept that?"

"Not until the other night at your place when you started to tell me about how you thought that maybe you'd fallen in love with John because he did have the spirit of adventure." Steve touched the scar on his face and stared at the floor. "For a moment there I sort of had hope that maybe you could feel the same way about me. But before I could say anything, you went on about how a man's being truthful was so important to you."

"And you decided that I wouldn't forgive you for that."

Steve raised his head and stared deeply into her eyes. "Would you?"

Summyr's throat tightened until she could hardly breath.

"That's what I thought," he said, getting up from the chair and walking to the other end of the room. When he reached the head of the table, he turned to face Summyr. "Every time I lied to you or didn't tell you the whole truth, I had a good reason, a professional reason. But all the time I was doing it, I knew that I was giving away what could be the most important thing in my life. Being with you."

"Oh," she said weakly.

"And now that I've thoroughly messed things up, I'm asking you to forgive me. I know that's expecting a lot. And things are even worse than that because I've got to be completely honest with you: there's no way I'm going to take a job that's completely safe. Whatever I end up doing, it's going to be something that excites me. I'm not going to sit around in some job just so I can live long enough to collect a good pension. That's just not me."

"I know that," said Summyr.

Steve nodded and came back to sit down next to her. He took her hand.

"I'll never lie to you again. I'm in love with you, Summyr. I've been in love with you since I first saw you in class."

Summyr gave a nervous laugh. "That was only a week ago. Are you sure?"

"Absolutely. And I'm willing to bet that you'll come to love me if you'll give us half a chance. What do you say?"

Summyr leaned forward until her face was close to Steve's.

"Let's risk it," she whispered just before her lips met his.

Chapter Sixteen

A month later, Summyr stood in the future home of Centered Self Yoga Studio. She was holding paint samples in her hand and trying to imagine what the whole space would look like painted sky blue. New windows had already been installed, and the plaster walls repaired. All that remained was the painting, which Summyr had offered to do herself to save money, and the installation of new carpeting. That she would leave to the experts. There could be no skimping on cost there, a yoga studio had to have the best carpet the owners could afford.

Just as Summyr began mentally calculating how much that might cost, Janet came up the stairs.

"Worrying about cost again?" she asked in a teasing voice. "Whenever I see you standing in the middle of the room with that frown on your face, I know exactly what's bothering you."

"Well, I have to. You don't seem worried about how long it's going to take you to recoup your investment here."

Janet gave her shoulder a squeeze. "Watching you and Chrissy, and how excited you are about all this, is almost repayment enough. But don't feel guilty, I fully intend to make my investment work. Frank didn't just leave me his money, he also left me some of his business sense. I intend to take full advantage of both."

Summyr smiled. "Okay, I'll try to remember that. How are things going downstairs?"

"The last I looked Chrissy was discussing where she wanted the walls put with this really cute young carpenter. And he seemed to be paying a lot more attention to her than to the blueprints."

"She's like a new person since she left Root and Branch," Summyr said.

"And she'll only come more alive as time goes by, I expect. Speaking of Root and Branch, have you been past there this week?"

Summyr shook her head.

"They're closed. I guess Richie wasn't up to the job. Without Chrissy, they didn't last a month."

"Having less competition will certainly help us get started," said Summyr, "although I never like to see a business fail."

"Neither do I, but the owners didn't do their job. You can't put a store in the hands of an inexperienced manager and expect the place to run itself. They should have been more involved in the day-to-day supervision."

Summyr nodded and held up a color sample. "Speaking of owner supervision, what do you think of this shade of blue for the walls?"

Janet squinted at the color, then at the room.

"Might work."

"Not too light."

"I'd go with a shade darker," Janet said, pointing at the next sample.

Summyr nodded. "I think so, too. I'm going to get the paint this afternoon."

"Aren't you teaching a class?"

Summyr nodded. "I'll run over there right after."

Janet glanced around the room. "I bet you'll be happy to get out of that warehouse."

"Yes. But it was really fortunate that they delayed their renovations after Schuster was implicated in the search for that embezzlement money. But they've got a new contractor in place now, so I'll have to be out by the end of next month."

"Don't worry. You'll make it with time to spare," said Janet. "By the way, I managed to rent that downstairs office in the back."

"That's great! Now the whole building is rented. What kind of business is going in there?"

Janet gave an exaggerated frown. "Well, I had some reservations about the guy running it. But after all, money is money."

"What is it?" Summyr asked with a sinking heart.

There was the sound of footsteps coming up the stairs.

"That's probably the new renter now. I'll let him explain it to you himself."

Without saying another word, Janet left the room and went down the stairs.

As Summyr watched her leave, Steve came into the room. He walked over and gave Summyr a hug.

"Has Janet broken the news?" he asked, smiling.

"As usual she's only given me part of the story," Summyr replied. "I guess you're renting the space downstairs, but whatever for?"

"Remember my friend who worked on the Peterson case with me?"

"The guy who's such a computer whiz?"

Steve nodded. "Well, we're going into business together doing private investigations. We'll handle mostly insurance fraud and some white collar crimes. Maybe missing persons now and then. He'll do the computer stuff and I'll do the legwork."

Before she could think, Summyr asked, "Will it be dangerous?"

He took her by both shoulders and turned her to face him. "I promised that I would never lie to you again, and I won't. There is always some risk when you're dealing with criminals. But I can assure you that I'll never take any foolish chances. If things start looking really bad, then I'll . . ." he paused for a moment, then laughed. "I'll call the police. How's that?"

Summyr smiled in relief, then gave him a quick kiss. "Good luck in your new business."

"Yeah. It's funny, isn't it, how we're all starting on something new. You and I and Chrissy and Janet: all starting new jobs."

"And you and I and Janet and my uncle, we're all starting on something new in a different way as well," Summyr said. "And so is my father. Don't forget that in two weeks you're going to a wedding with me down in Florida."

"I've already made room in my schedule," Steve said with a grin.

"Good. Make sure you pay attention while you're there, since there's likely to be one coming up in your future."

Steve grinned. "I'll make a point of it."

Summyr walked over to the large front window that gave her a panoramic view of the main street of Eastfield. Steve came over and stood by her side. He put an arm around her.

"What are you thinking?" he asked.

"That it's funny, how on the surface this town never seems any different, yet all the time changes are happening. Old things come to an end, and new things begin. It's the changes you don't see that make the most difference."

Steve gave her a long, deep kiss.

"What was that for?" Summyr asked.

"That was for new beginnings."

"Ah, well, I'm all in favor of that," she replied, pressing her lips to his.